PRAISE FOR SUE MISSING

"A tense and suspenseful page-turner! 192 Days Missing by Sue Denver is the second book in her exciting paranormal detective series featuring werewolf Sara Flores. Fast-paced, with a sense of danger and urgency, this was hard to put down. The mystery is well-plotted and tight, but we also see the team gel and are introduced to a fabulous new character in Judy. Judy is a middle-aged and quirky badass in her own formidable way, and I loved seeing that representation here, particularly in action-packed crime fiction! I love paranormal and shifter books and how Denver uses Sara's werewolf abilities in this story. Denver does not shy away from some of the more horrific aspects of the story, which had me all in for Sara going full werewolf! But Denver also balances this out with humor, and there are several laugh-out-loud moments throughout. I stayed up way past bedtime to finish!"

— READTHISANDSTEEP, INSTAGRAM

"*192 Days Missing* is compulsively readable. I loved the development of the bond between Sara and her team, the banter with Mason, the one-upmanship between Connor and Sara, and the sheer force of nature that is Judy (and as an older woman myself, I appreciated the portrayal of an older woman as savvy and sexy). Once again, Denver dragged me into Sara's world and kept me up way too late."

— MJ SILVERSMITH, DISCOVERY

"It's all fun and games (and a regular day at your 9-5 job), until you are abducted from a parking garage, just to find out that you weren't the target and you might die if you don't prove yourself useful to the kidnappers (that kill women for fun). And if you think this isn't curious enough to be interested in this book, just ask yourself why would a werewolf want to learn Krav Maga?"

"If you want to read about billionaires getting justice for their crimes, with a badass, stubborn, woman werewolf, and a team that make her life a living semi-hell (because she is a loner), then grab this beauty of a book. The ending is really cool, seriously, this book only grows better. Awesome stuff here."

— SCRIBBLE'S WORTH BOOK REVIEWS

192 DAYS MISSING

A SARA FLORES, WEREWOLF P.I. NOVEL

SUE DENVER

JGF PRESS

192 Days Missing by Sue Denver, at SueDenver.com and WolfLady.net

Published by JGF Press, at JGFpress.com

Copyright © 2023 by Sue Denver, All rights reserved.

No part of this book may be reproduced in any form or by any electronic or mechanical means, including information storage and retrieval systems, without written permission from the author, except for the use of brief quotations in a book review.

It should go without saying, given this is a book about a werewolf, but just in case(!)... This book is a work of fiction. Names, characters, places, and incidents are a product of the author's imagination. Real locales and public and celebrity names are sometimes used for atmospheric purposes. Any resemblance to actual people, living or dead, or to businesses, companies, tribes, events, institutions, or places, is either coincidental or used in a fictional manner.

Cover art: © Photo Spirit, Shutterstock

Published June 14, 2023 by JGF Press, Crossville TN

CONTENTS

Sara Flores' world	vii
Prologue	1
Chapter 1	5
Chapter 2	9
Chapter 3	12
Chapter 4	17
Chapter 5	23
Chapter 6	26
Chapter 7	31
Chapter 8	35
Chapter 9	38
Chapter 10	42
Chapter 11	46
Chapter 12	53
Chapter 13	55
Chapter 14	60
Chapter 15	62
Chapter 16	69
Chapter 17	73
Chapter 18	77
Chapter 19	79
Chapter 20	84
Chapter 21	88
Chapter 22	94
Chapter 23	100
Chapter 24	106
Chapter 25	109
Chapter 26	112
Chapter 27	116
Chapter 28	123
Chapter 29	128
Chapter 30	133
Chapter 31	135
Chapter 32	141

Chapter 33	144
Chapter 34	153
Chapter 35	156
Chapter 36	162
Chapter 37	166
Chapter 38	172
Chapter 39	178
Chapter 40	186
Chapter 41	192
Chapter 42	194
Chapter 43	198
Chapter 44	204
Chapter 45	207
Chapter 46	212
Chapter 47	219
Chapter 48	226
About the Author	233
Also by Sue Denver	235
Acknowledgments	239

SARA FLORES' WORLD

- Sara's world is our everyday, normal world.
- Nobody believes in werewolves, vampires or anything supernatural.
- Sara was turned into a werewolf by her former neighbor Joe White Wolf — right before he died.
- Sara thinks she's the only werewolf on earth, but she hopes (or fears) she's wrong.
- Lupiti elders remember their grandfathers talk about seeing old Joe White Wolf turn into a wolf during tribal ceremonies — way back in the late 1800's.
- This tells Sara she may have a very, very long life — if her new lifestyle doesn't get her killed.

PROLOGUE

192 Days Earlier
Lupiti, Oklahoma

A laska Brown no longer noticed all the security cameras at Tulsa's Four Leaf Clover Casino. She knew they were in the parking lot where she parked, in the cashier's cage where she worked, and in the casino restaurant where she got dinner. That didn't even count the five cameras each at the many, many gaming tables.

As far as she knew, the only place on casino property without cameras was inside the bathrooms.

She believed they'd have cameras there, too, if it weren't illegal.

She awakened at 11:30 that morning, the 17th of September, as though it were a normal day instead of what was to become the worst day of her life.

She looked outside and saw the thermometer showing 81 degrees, which made her smile. Finally — a little relief from what had been a brutal summer.

She checked to make sure her daughter Macey had left for high school and winced at the clothes Macey had left strewn on her bed. She told herself to leave them — Macey needed to learn responsibility. But... "Maybe next time," she said as she picked them up and put them back on hangers.

She opened the door to Ricky's room and gave a short sigh. He wouldn't be home from college until Thanksgiving — which seemed years away. She made a mental note to look for a book he'd like when she had her dinner break. She could send it to him.

Alaska started two cups of coffee brewing, then stared at her wardrobe. She only had two suits, so she switched them each day. Yesterday was the yellow one, so today it would have to be the blue one. But she paired it with a pink blouse instead of the white she had worn two days ago.

She tightened her mouth. She needed to look professional so she got that promotion her boss was dangling. But he always dressed so sharply and she'd seen him noticing how she dressed. Maybe she needed to find the money — somehow — for another suit?

Alaska downed one cup of coffee — half sugar — before putting on her makeup. She poured the second cup in her to-go mug for her trip into Tulsa. The drive time wasn't wasted — she always used it to talk to her mom. To make sure she and her dad were doing okay. It was the "special treat" part of her day.

As usual, her shift in the cashiers' cage ended at 10 PM that night. As she stepped into the exit elevator for the parking lot, Alaska assumed cameras were still following her.

As the doors were closing, a gorgeous young woman jumped in. She had long black hair and looked a little like Alaska's daughter Macey. Alaska nodded at her. She'd seen the girl a few times and knew she worked as a cocktail server.

Alaska followed her out onto the fourth parking level but stopped when she saw the girl looking around, confused. She was staring at the letters and numbers on the columns and looking down at her phone.

"Do you know where you're parked?" Alaska asked her.

The girl shook her head. "My boyfriend texted me he's parked at B-15. Do you know where that is?"

"That's right next to where I park. Come on, I'll show you." She walked the girl down a row and around a corner to where her used Honda Fit awaited.

"There," she said, pointing at a column. "B-15."

Alaska didn't notice two vans stopped nearby. She had no way of knowing they were positioned exactly to block the views of the only two cameras covering this section.

She did notice when a man opened the side door on one of the vans. She turned to look at him.

There was another noise — behind her. Before she could turn, a hand from behind slapped over her mouth, an arm grabbed her around the waist, and Alaska's feet came off the ground.

She saw the other man grab the girl, and both of them were rushed to the open van door.

It happened so fast!

Alaska struggled and kicked and belatedly opened her mouth to scream. The man holding her grabbed the inside of her right arm and pinched. The pain was excruciating. Tears sprang to her eyes. She stopped moving — hoping that would stop the pain.

Alaska was tossed into the back of the van on a carpeted floor, then re-grabbed by the same man. He pulled her up against him, holding her with an arm tight on her waist and a hand back over her mouth.

"What the hell?" asked the driver, turning to look at them. Alaska saw only a ball cap pulled low, sunglasses, and a turtleneck sweater pulled up over his chin.

"They were together," said the man holding Alaska. "Can't leave one behind."

"Shit."

The van door closed, blocking out all light except what came from the front. The driver turned back around, and the van started moving.

Alaska heard gasping and turned to look at the girl. Her eyes were huge and her chest was moving in and out — fast. She was struggling to breathe. Alaska saw her panic as she wheezed and struggled desperately to get air in her lungs.

The man holding the girl — a sunburned white goon with buzz-cut hair so white it disappeared on his skull — let go of her and shook his head.

"What's wrong with her?"

Alaska grabbed at the fingers covering her mouth. The guy holding her let her speak.

"She's having an asthma attack. Let me help her."

The van jolted to a stop.

"You can help her?" asked the man behind the wheel.

Alaska nodded.

"Help her and I might not have to kill you today."

Alaska stared at him in horror.

"We didn't come for you. Show us you're useful, and you might survive. For a time."

1

Sara Flores
The Downtown Dojo in Tulsa, Oklahoma
Current day

I knew this was a bad idea.

My name is Sara Flores, and I'm both a private investigator and a werewolf. The werewolf part of me wasn't normally a problem. I guarded that secret like it meant my life — because it probably did.

But today Connor Rockwood was making it a problem.

He had dragged me to this dojo on the eighth floor of a low-rent office building in Tulsa, Oklahoma. The owner is one of his former Special Forces buddies who lets him use the place for workouts when no classes are scheduled.

Outside I saw lightning. Strong winds drove the rain horizontally — right at the windows. It was one of those angry March storms that like to blow through Tulsa and scurry the residents into hiding.

The dojo was a simple place, with a huge blue mat in the center of the room surrounded by banged-up green lockers for changing, a wall rack of bo fighting sticks, and three orange benches, one of which I was sitting on.

It was my fault I was here. Working with Connor had seemed like a good idea two months ago. That's when I became a private investigator licensed by the state of Oklahoma. Fifty-five hours of classes, pass a test — and voila! — I'm a private eye.

I wanted the license to back off suspicious cops who might find me near dead bodies in parts of town no sane woman would go near. The license gave me an excuse to be there.

And, yes, I've been in the vicinity of a bunch of dead bodies in the two years since I was turned by my neighbor, a dying Lupiti shaman. Don't get me wrong — I'm happy he did it. But the man told me nothing. As far as I know, I'm the only werewolf — the only supernatural anything — on the planet.

As for the dead bodies — finding missing or threatened innocents has become my calling, and the assholes who take them aren't interested in giving them up. Not without a fight.

"C'mon, Flores." Connor grabbed my arm and dragged me out on the mat. We were both in street clothes but barefoot.

"You can't learn Krav Maga up here, darlin'." He pointed to my head. "Your body has to learn it too." He had a slight Tennessee accent that normally made me smile since it came from a body built like the Hulk.

Today I wasn't smiling.

"I'm not paying you to teach me martial arts," I said, surprised at how defensive I sounded. "I have a brown belt. What I want is all the street-fighting strategy you learned in Special Forces."

"That's what I'm tryin' to teach you."

He eyed me, pursing his lips. "Big, bad, brown belt, huh? Show me some moves."

My eyes narrowed. If he smiled, I was going to have to kill him.

This was a very bad idea.

I'd met Connor two months ago, when I hired him to bodyguard my very first client. She'd been run off the road and had her house bombed by a man determined to kill her. I'd stashed the two of us in a hotel suite and hired Connor to protect her while I was asleep.

He'd done a good job — apparently in more ways than one since my client was now dating him.

Connor reached across the three feet between us and pushed my shoulder. Provoking me.

I took the push without moving my feet and imagined him with a big wolf-sized bite out of his shoulder. I was careful not to smile.

He threw up his hands. "This is a bad idea."

Well... at least we agreed on that.

"Just teach me the moves," I said, also throwing up my hands. "What's with you? You want us to spar? You're eight inches taller than me, outweigh me by more than 100 pounds, and you're a man. And former Special Forces. What are you trying to prove?"

"And who d'you think you'll be fighting — teenage girls?"

I wanted to scream.

I'd *love* to test myself against Connor — because I didn't know who would win. And I need to know because the next man trying to kill me might have his skills. My life might depend on it. Thanks to my wolf, I've been stronger than any man I've gone up against in the two years since my transformation. But none of them were at Connor's skill level.

The problem is, Connor would know immediately there was something wrong about me. Beaten — or almost beaten — by a woman? He'd never let that go without answers. Thus far, only three people know what I am. They're all my friends, but it makes my skin crawl that they know.

No way I'm adding Connor to that list.

He snapped his fingers in front of my eyes. "This won't work. You can't teach heart or guts. And you, little girl, don't have either."

I smiled. He was still trying to provoke me, but I was immune to macho posturing.

He raised his eyebrows. "You reckon that's funny? Your next client won't think so when you get her killed because you can't protect her."

I lunged forward and punched my right fist — twisting it in perfect karate form — aiming directly at his throat.

I wasn't aware I was moving until my fist was almost there, and, horrified, I tried to stop.

Connor got his forearm up to block me — he'd been expecting

something, after all. My fist hit his forearm and I heard a very faint crack.

We broke apart.

He grabbed his left forearm, his eyes wide in surprise.

I grabbed my right hand. Instead of a soft neck, my knuckles had hit bone and I'd broken at least two of them. The pain was so bad it made my eyes water, but I had to hide it. Tomorrow my knuckles would be healed. No way to explain that except that they were never damaged.

I bent over until the urge to scream in pain stopped.

"I'm sorry," I said. "I moved before I thought. I didn't think you could get to me. What did you say...."

Connor moved the fingers on his damaged arm and winced. He looked back at me, evaluating.

"My fault," he said. "Nothing worked. Saying you'd get a client killed — I went too far. But — hell, Flores. That was so fast I barely saw it. And strong."

"You have pain moving some of those fingers, don't you?"

He stared at me.

"I have really good hearing and I heard a crack. I think your ulna is fractured."

He kept staring at me.

I closed my eyes. Fractures take a long time to heal. Time he wouldn't be able to do his normal bodyguard work.

All my fault.

I walked over to the bench and picked up Connor's cell phone.

"Stick your thumb on here so I can call Judy. She'll get you checked out." I turned away from him to dial, hiding the broken knuckles on my hand.

"Judy? It's Sara. Could you do a job for me? Connor needs the best orthopedic guy in Tulsa. His ulna bone is fractured — hopefully just a hairline."

I handed the phone back to Connor and left.

I could feel his eyes on my back.

2

Sara Flores
Office building in Tulsa

"I've got a new client for us," said Mason Spencer, my 23-year-old tech genius and business partner.

We were in my spartan one-room office in downtown Tulsa, which had one desk, no computer, and three crappy chairs — one behind my desk and two in front. There was nothing on the plain, white walls, and the floors were a fake-wood laminate.

Mason was seated across from me. His feet, in bright orange running shoes, rested on a Salvation Army coffee table.

Mason has very long brown hair, which you probably wouldn't notice in Pennsylvania — because there he wears it pulled back tight. He grew up in State College, where his German father teaches college math. When Mason visits Tulsa and his mother's Lupiti tribe, he's more likely to wear it loose. Like it was now.

Mason had flown here to wire up my new office for maximum security — both from physical and electronic break-ins.

Mason was one of my first rescues two years ago. Now, in addition to being my partner, he was also my friend. Mason knew I was a werewolf because I'd had to transform to save his life. He was the only person alive I trusted.

"A new client?" I asked.

He nodded. "My mother had them call me. They don't have any money, so we'll have to use some of those "donations" we have to handle it."

We both smiled. Two of our previous rescues required going against very rich, very evil men. Both of them had offshore bank accounts that Mason had emptied and put into our accounts. They wouldn't be needing the money any longer, being dead.

We called them our "donors." Using their money to rescue other victims would never make up for the lives they took — but it would have pissed the hell out of each of them. That gave us some satisfaction.

Mason looked at his watch. "They should be here in 10 minutes."

Good, I thought. *I could use a new client.*

"You need a new client," Mason said as if he could read my brain, "so you'll stop beating yourself up about Connor's broken arm."

"I am *not* beating myself up...."

"Really? It was a hairline fracture. Connor should be used to getting beat up in his line of work. And fighting you? He's lucky that's all it was."

"He can't *work*, Mason. Two months at least. And it's my fault."

"Well then, you'll have to hire him to help with this investigation."

"You... I... what?"

"Cat got your tongue?"

"Very funny." My eyes narrowed as I looked at him. "This better be a real client and not some made up thing to get him on our team. You know I didn't want to hire him in the first place. I'm not sure we need him."

Mason's face went dark and he sighed. "The clients are very real."

He got up and opened the tiny refrigerator, which I stocked with water and Diet Coke. He pulled out two of the latter and threw one to me.

"I don't know how you stand this swill," he said, opening his.

"Like your Mountain Dew is better. At least this doesn't have flame retardant in it."

We glared at each other. Then we started laughing.

I never had a younger brother. Never had any kind of sibling. But maybe this was what it was like?

There was a knock on the door.

3

Sara Flores
Office building in Tulsa

It was awkward.
  The office lacked a fourth chair, so I ended up sitting on the edge of the desk. Mason sat with the couple — Dyani and George Stintson. They looked more at him than at me.
  He'd probably had to talk them into coming here.
  The only surprise was neither of them looked Lupiti. I'd thought Mason was bringing me clients from his tribe.
  George was in a rumpled gray suit, tie, and glasses, with a thick mane of silver hair. Behind his glasses, George had the thousand-yard stare I'd seen once on a woman I'd "rescued" too late. She'd checked out of her life because the horror was too much to take.
  George didn't offer to shake hands, so neither did I.
  Dyani had coal-black hair fluffed out on her shoulders, but the wrinkles on her face said the hair was probably dyed. The skin around her eyes had that bruised look you get when you haven't slept well in too long to remember, and there was red in her eyes from crying. But her mouth was pursed. She was deeply, deeply angry.

Whatever had happened to these two, it wasn't recent. But neither was it over.

"How can I help you?" I asked.

"Our daughter — Alaska — is missing," said George. Then he shut his mouth and his eyes lost focus. Apparently, that was all he came to say.

I looked at Mason.

He said, "Dyani, give her the picture of Alaska."

She looked at him, and for a minute I thought she might refuse. Finally she opened her purse and pulled out a picture. She looked at Mason again, as though still deciding, then held it out in my direction. She kept her eyes on Mason.

I removed my butt from the desk and took the photo.

"Her last name?"

Mason answered. "It's Alaska Brown."

I looked at the picture. Alaska was smiling in it, showing apple cheeks and long, black hair. She looked to be in her late 30s.

George and Dyani remained silent. Not looking at me.

"How long has she been missing?" I asked.

Dyani raised her head. "Six months."

"What do the police say?"

"They can't find her. They're not even looking anymore."

George's eyes had suddenly focused on me. "Our Alaska has been missing for 192 days." He paused, making sure I understood the full impact of missing a daughter for that long.

"Why aren't the police looking?"

"They say she's an adult," Dyani said. "They say she probably went off with a boyfriend, and she can disappear if she wants to. It's just a way of not having to look for her."

I raised an eyebrow. Dyani narrowed her eyes. "She has two beautiful children. A son Ricky who is in college in California, and a daughter Macey who's 17. Alaska would never have abandoned her children. Never."

George nodded his head. "Children are life to us. She would not have done this."

I looked at them. I wasn't sure how to say this.

Dyani nodded. "You think she must be dead. The police think if she didn't leave voluntarily, then she's dead. Or hiding from us. But... she *might* be alive. Held some place — where she can't contact us. We have to know."

"So," said George. "What will you do about this?"

I looked at Mason. He nodded. I turned to the couple.

"If we do this, I will send you a contract to sign, and you will give me $1, so you are officially our clients. But... before you say yes, I want you to know something.

"Mason and I are fortunate that we can take only those cases where it matters to us. But because we care, we won't stop once we take it. No matter where it leads. The majority of missing or murdered women are taken by someone close to them. It could be a relative of yours. A good friend. This could add more devastation to your lives."

Dyani looked at her husband. He nodded. She turned to me and said, "We need to know."

"Also," I said, "if she did go voluntarily and she's okay but doesn't want contact with you, we'll honor that. We'll tell you she's alive and well, but not how to find her."

"Fine," Dyani said. "Because that won't be the case."

George looked at Mason. Then back at me. "Do you think you can find her?"

"I don't know," I admitted. "Six months is a long time. But unlike the police Mason and I will give you all our time. You'll be our only client. Mason is a genius at computers, and I can read people. We have found others who have disappeared. Not all of them were alive, but we found them. We will try our best for you."

They nodded.

"One last question. Is there anyone you suspect? Anyone who hated Alaska or liked her too much. Anyone you think knows more than they're telling?"

They looked at each other for a long moment but shook their heads.

"Okay," I said, "If not suspect... is there anyone we should make sure to talk to in order to rule out?"

Dyani looked at George. "Joe Bob?" she asked him. He nodded and she turned to me.

"Joe Bob Morton. He owns JB's Liquor store."

I looked at her, waiting for a reason.

"Alaska reported him to the police. He was letting underage kids buy beer, maybe more, out the back of his store. She caught Ricky with some...."

"He's a good boy," her husband said. "But boys like to test limits."

Dyani nodded.

"What happened with Joe Bob?"

"He lost a lot of money — a big fine. And they threatened his liquor license."

George added, "The cops drive by his place all the time, so he's scared to sell to kids anymore."

I asked, "How long ago was this?"

Dyani said, "About a year and a half before Alaska disappeared."

We shook hands, then Mason showed them out.

He came back, and we sat at the coffee table. I shook my head. "I can't imagine what it must be like for them..."

"Me either."

"We're not set up for this," I told him. "We don't have a client contract to send them. We haven't needed one before. There are piles and piles of paperwork crap we're going to need to be official private investigators."

"I'll bet Judy could have an excellent first draft for us in an hour."

I twisted my mouth. "We're using her too much. There must be some other way to get all this admin stuff done."

Mason tilted his head. "I'm listening. What's your other way to do it?"

"I don't know!" I slammed my hand down on the chair. "But Mason — everyone we bring in is a risk."

"That they could find out about you?"

"Yes, that too. But mainly it risks their lives. We're not going after Sunday school teachers here."

Mason and I sat there. Thinking. It seemed pointless, since all our thinking for the past month hadn't solved this problem.

15

Mason shrugged his shoulders. "We've got a ton of bureaucracy junk we need done right now. I'm not going to do it. You're not going to do it. Let's get Judy to set things up. Maybe after that we can figure something else out."

I sighed. "You're right. We need her now. We can reevaluate in a month or two."

Mason pulled out his phone and swiped then tapped it. "Okay, I'm recording. Say that again."

I frowned. "Say what?"

"That I was right."

I wadded up a piece of paper from the coffee table and threw it at him.

4

Sara Flores
Office building in Tulsa

I scheduled a meeting for the next morning, nine AM, here in my office. At Mason's insistence, I invited both Judy Street and Connor Rockwood. I had agreed with his reasons yesterday; but now, as the time approached, I wanted out.

For one thing, the office just wasn't big enough. We had one tiny room, three chairs and four people. And there was a four-foot rack of clothes standing against one side of the room. It held the outfits, wigs, and disguises I might need at a moment's notice.

Besides, business meetings were crap. I could picture the four of us — all sitting around the table, each posturing about our expertise, one-upping each other.

I'd seen this kind of game before.

I had vowed never *ever* to work in an office again. During my five-year, ill-conceived marriage, I'd been the office manager for a regional publishing company. You can't imagine the egos I dealt with. One ad manager had come to me furious — demanding I switch his office with another manager's. He'd measured both offices and determined his was two inches smaller than the other guy's. That was the day I lost it. I told him two inches would matter if they were on his dick — but not in his office. I was out of a job two hours later.

I smiled, remembering. I hadn't then.

Mason walked in.

"You're smiling," he noted. "I thought you'd be ready to scratch my eyes out."

He'd been to see the Stintsons and he handed me the signed contract. "I made copies of the rest." He put a little packet of paper in four places on the coffee table. A photo of Alaska was on top of each.

"Mason..."

He looked at me and shook his head. "No. You know this makes sense or you'd never have agreed to it. Suck it up, Sara. It's all about the client. Right?"

I hate him when he's right.

There was a knock at the door and Judy came in — carrying a folding chair. It was one of the things I most disliked about her. Not just that she was better organized than me or Mason. That didn't count — she was better organized than anyone else in the world. But she was always a step ahead of me — seeing a need and solving it before I had to ask.

I know it sounds petty. It *is* petty. But it's damn humbling, and I don't do humble very well.

"Y'all need a name on the door," she said.

"Why?"

Judy rolled her eyes at me. "You fixin' to look like you're any good at this private investigator stuff?"

She turned away from my gaping-mouth look and winked at Mason. She pulled out four packets of papers from her briefcase and stuck one packet under each of the piles Mason had on the table.

Judy was a mystery to me. She was in her 50s with fluffy gray hair and more makeup than I've ever worn in my life. She also wore low necklines and flirted with every man I've ever seen her meet.

And they flirted back.

We met her through our first official client, who told us that underneath the fluff Judy could browbeat contractors — or anyone else — until they moved faster than was even possible. Mason hired her last month to do all our travel plans. He marveled at how easy she made it for him.

And, I had to admit, my one phone call to her two nights ago had fixed everything for Connor.

The chair was a nice touch too. But when I looked at her, I just saw a potential victim. I didn't want her life to be my responsibility.

Another knock and Connor came in. At 6' 4" and 240 pounds he immediately made the room feel crowded. He was the only one dressed in a suit, although he carried his jacket. His right shirt sleeve was unbuttoned because the brace on his forearm strained the material.

I winced with guilt.

I took a deep breath and let it out. Time to do this thing. Time to find Alaska.

We sat at the four chairs and I gave them the overview. Alaska Stintson, age 39 at disappearance — on September 17 of last year. Missing 192 — now 193 — days. Black hair. Brown eyes. 5' 6". Weight 120. No tattoos. One horizontal C-section scar almost three inches, right above the pubic hairline.

Alaska was last seen walking to her car with another casino employee — Brittany Rebane. Rebane had just quit her job and left with her boyfriend for Mexico, where the two of them were taking a year to camp and sightsee.

The Tulsa cops interviewed Rebane from Mexico and she said Alaska got into a van with a man she seemed to know. Willingly. It was why the cops weren't really investigating.

That was the last anyone saw or heard from Alaska.

All of us looked at her photo. I picked up my pile and looked at what Judy had added to it.

"Judy?"

She nodded. "Some background. Each year 600,000 people go missing in the U.S. Most are solved within the first year. But the others... in Oklahoma, right now, there are 252 unsolved cases.

"Four things are key for how likely they are to be found: 1) How short a time they've been missing, 2) How young they are, 3) The people-density of their location — medium is best, and 4) if they're female."

"Medium density?" I asked.

"Rural or big cities are the worst for finding someone."

"Women are more likely to be found than missing men?"

"Yes," said Judy. "But that's because a lot of them are found dead."

"And one more thing. Alaska is white, but she lives in Lupiti. She doesn't really look native, but she has long black hair. There's a huge problem of missing native women. There are organizations formed to fight the problem. They use MMIW — which stands for Missing and Murdered Indigenous Women. You might run into this, so I printed out some of their work."

Okay, I admitted to myself — she thinks like an investigator.

Connor hadn't said a word during the meeting. "Connor?"

Judy said, "Connor's the strong silent type, aren't you sweetie?"

Connor smiled at her and then glowered at me. "I'm not sure what my role is here."

"I've got a little undercover work for you — and Judy — if you're interested."

Judy nodded. Connor was unreadable.

"Fair enough," I said. "I will be interviewing people at the casino where Alaska worked. But I don't want to walk in blind — or I could miss something.

"Judy, how about you drop in at the Four Leaf Casino. Shoot craps. Play blackjack. Try slot machines. Do you know how to gamble?"

Judy shook her head no.

"Even better — you can ask people for advice on it. Also, chat up the employees. Ask some of them if it's a good place to work. Mainly get a feel for what's normal there as well as anything that feels off — in the customers, the employees, or the operations."

Judy nodded. Then she smiled. "Do Connor and I have to report our winnings?" She winked at Connor.

I rolled my eyes. "Just deduct them from your more substantial losses on an expense report."

I sighed and added, "An expense report you'll have to first design for us."

I looked at Connor. "Do you think a casino would want to hire a guy with your superior credentials — if it was just for a month or two while your arm keeps you out of regular bodyguard work? It's a perfect excuse why you'd consider it. But would they?"

Connor tilted back on his chair, thinking. I crossed my fingers that the cheap chair wouldn't splinter holding 240 pounds on its two thin back legs.

He finally brought the chair back down and nodded. "Maybe. You want me to get inside their security? Look for holes?"

I nodded.

"Then what?"

"That depends on what you find. Will you try it?"

He agreed.

We broke up the meeting soon afterwards, but I asked Connor to stay. I perched, half sitting on the front of my desk. Connor leaned back against a wall. Guess neither of us wanted to be in a seat while the other was standing.

"I appreciate your willingness to help us on this case," I said. "People at the casino are some of our most-likely suspects. If their security or top management is involved, it'll be dangerous for you. So watch yourself in there."

He tilted his head and looked at me as if I were an idiot.

I rubbed my eyes with my fingers, then ran them through my hair. "Just let me finish so I can sleep better at night. Then you can yell at me."

He waved his hand, telling me to go ahead.

"Given your size and your background, anyone who wants you gone is going to go at you sideways. A pat on the back with a needle in the hand. A handshake. Something in your food or drink. It'll be sneaky and they'll be good at it. Because if they're coming after you, they've already had practice in disappearing people."

He rolled his eyes. "I've got 20 years in Special Forces plus 11 as an executive bodyguard."

I raised both hands in surrender. "Okay. Okay. Don't expect me to cry over you if you do something stupid and get yourself killed. Mason would feel bad, though."

"Mason?"

"He thinks you'd make a good member of our team, going forward. Full or part-time. Whatever you'd like."

"But you don't?"

I shrugged my shoulders. "He's probably right — we could often use your skills. But hell, Connor, I've always been a lone wolf. I like being on my own. I can barely stand working with Mason. Anyone else makes my skin crawl."

He laughed. It was a good laugh. "I might do the P.I. thing one day," he said. "But probably open my own shop. Not work for..." He trailed off.

"A woman?" I asked with a smirk.

"*Anyone* else. No offense meant."

"None taken. You're an alpha male. You want to be the boss."

Connor frowned. "I don't have chain of command problems. But..." He shrugged. "I reckon that's close enough."

He came forward. "I'll go get hired by the casino."

He slapped me on the back as he walked past me to the door.

"Gotcha," he said with a grin. "Guess you'd better give *yourself* that talk about sneak attacks." He closed the door on any reply I could make.

I rubbed my eyes again. "Men," I muttered. But I smiled.

5

Judy Street
Four Leaf Clover Casino

J udy paused just inside the entrance of the Four Leaf Clover Casino and took in the sensory overload. Flashing multi-colored lights were everywhere. Noises — Ka-chings, thumping, bells, sirens — assaulted her eardrums. Everything moved. Cards were flipping, rollers were rolling, dragons were snorting fire, cars were racing — all on huge electronic machines twice the size of a big man.

In front of the machines were human beings. Feeding in money.

Judy walked down the rows of these games. Nobody looked at her. Nobody talked to anyone else. Nobody looked away from their games except to find another bill to feed into the hungry machine mouths.

And why was nobody smiling?

If gambling was fun, why was everybody staring at the screens as if they were watching very old reruns on TV?

This would not do.

Judy found a restroom and looked at herself in the mirror. She ran her fingers up and through her gray — silver, she corrected herself — Meg Ryan hair, mussing it so it looked like she might have just crawled out of bed. She used a fingernail, with Kiss-Me-Tangerine nail polish, to remove a little smudge of mascara on a lower lid. She added lipgloss and a little blush in the low "V" of her neckline.

Not bad at all for 56, she decided.

Back in the lounge, she spotted an available game right next to an attractive older man and plunked herself down in front of it. She had to lean way back to see all the machine.

Understanding it? She hadn't a clue. There were circles and numbers and stars all over it — nothing made any sense. What kind of game was it?

There were only two clear things anywhere on the game — the slot that took your bills and a big button that said, "play." No levers. No other buttons. If this was a game, it made no sense.

She gave a big — exaggerated — sigh and turned to the man on her right. He was watching lights jumping all over his machine. When they stopped, he turned to look at her.

She said, "I must be dumb as bricks, honey, because I don't have a clue how to play this. Do you?"

His eyes looked her over, and he smiled. "Dumb as bricks is who they make these things for. You put in your money, you press the button, you watch the light show, and you lose. Once in awhile you win, and you get a little ticket like these." He showed her a stack of paper slips.

"You see those machines over there?" He pointed at a wall. She nodded.

"When you get tired, you go put your tickets in there and collect your pitiful winnings."

"That's it?"

He nodded.

She shook her head. "This isn't anything like I thought. I saw some poker tournaments on TV, and it looked more fun than this."

"Do you play poker?"

"Not yet."

"I'm willing to play it for awhile. You want to come watch?"

She smiled, and they both stood up. She linked her hand around his arm.

"Show me how to play poker."

One hour later, she still didn't understand poker. Oh, she had the rules down now. But there was subterranean stuff going on that was much harder to grasp. She could never tell if he would raise or fold based on the cards he held.

But it didn't matter that much. He was fun, and he seemed to like her a little ditsy.

Her answering service called her at 11:15, as she'd requested. She stepped away from the table to take the call and made herself look concerned. She hung up.

"Got to run, hon," she said. "Thanks for a fun evening. Maybe I'll see you around here another time?" She leaned forward and kissed him on the cheek.

She blew off his attempts to walk her out and flew outside to the private car she had waiting. Which Sara Flores would be paying for.

She settled back as the driver moved into traffic and considered what she'd learned. Jerry — the man she'd adopted for the night — thought the odds were slightly better at the Four Leaf than at other town casinos. She wasn't sure if that was important, but maybe.

What was important was personal security. She'd told Jerry she worried about her safety, as a woman in a casino. He'd assured her the Four Leaf was the safest because it was in a better part of town than the others, and the parking garage had better lighting.

However... He told her all the casinos have fewer security people than they did a few years back. In their parking lots and even in the casinos themselves. It was hard for them to find employees — nobody wanted to work late shifts.

She'd said, "What you really mean is they're too cheap to pay what's needed to hire more security employees. Right?"

He'd agreed.

So profits were more important to casinos than maintaining their former levels of customer safety. And if their customer safety had deteriorated, so had their employee safety.

Tomorrow she'd come back in the day and chat up some waitresses and bartenders. See how safe they felt working there.

6

Sara Flores
Lupiti Police Department

The Lupiti police department was housed in a concrete block building — all painted white. The outside had windows with multi-pane grids of reinforced steel.

I'd never been in here before, and I was very sorry to be in here now — inside *any* police station. My lungs were working harder than normal, as though the air inside had less oxygen than it was supposed to have. I could hear my heart speed up.

Coming here as a P.I., on behalf of a family, should not make me worry. But it took all my willpower not to run back outside the door and gulp down lots and lots of free air.

Freedom.

All wolves fear entrapment.

I had that fear plus another — the fear of being locked up by some government black ops group, so they could experiment on me. Maybe duplicate me as a new stealth weapon. Call me paranoid, but I'm quite sure if some groups found out I exist — I'd never be free again.

No black ops people here, I reassured myself. I forced my breathing to slow.

Inside was a solid wall blocking the entrance to the police desks. It had a single horizontal window in it — undoubtedly bullet-proof glass. A shaved-head bald officer sat there, typing into a computer that was faced away from the window.

Cops made my skin crawl.

Probably because of my guilty conscience. If they knew even one of the many, many ways I've broken the law in the past two years…

"Yes?"

The cop had slid back a panel of the window and was looking at me with his eyebrows raised.

Oh great, I thought. *Let's see how suspicious you can act while you're in here. Wouldn't that be smart?*

"Sorry," I said. "Daydreaming. I need to see the officer assigned to the Alaska Brown missing persons case."

"You are?"

"Sara Flores." I showed him my shield and handed him my card. "Private investigator…"

His lip curled and he looked like he'd spotted a cockroach.

"… hired by the family."

He uncurled his lip, slid the glass shut, nodded once, turned away, and picked up a phone.

I stood there watching. After hanging up the phone, the man turned sideways to his desk and started moving papers around. He didn't look at any of them long enough to be reading anything on them. He kept his body sideways and his head down — purposefully not looking at me.

No odors were coming through the glass, so I couldn't smell what was causing his behavior.

I played a "What's bugging him" game in my mind. Private eyes in general? Women in general? Me personally — at first sight? Although I couldn't imagine the latter. I was such a sweetheart.

A door opened at the far end of the wall. A handsome man, late 30s, with some native blood showing in his cheekbones and black hair, stuck his head out the door. He looked at me.

"You the P.I.?"

I nodded.

"I'm Sergeant Axel Walker. Come on back."

He held the door open. He was dressed casually in a light blue shirt with insignia paired with plain navy pants. He looked like he would have a killer smile — if he first caught up on a couple nights of sleep.

Somehow I doubted he was going to smile for me.

He led me to a small conference room. Crappy chairs. Beat-up table. Painted cement block walls. Really warm and homey.

To prevent as much hassle as possible, I immediately gave him a letter from the Stintsons saying I represent them as to their missing daughter Alaska and to please give me their full cooperation.

Axel Walker had more body control than the bald cop out front — he didn't curl his lip. He returned the letter.

"Can I see a copy of the file on Alaska?"

"No."

I waited, but it appeared that was all he planned to say.

"May I ask why?"

"You're not an officer of the law."

"No, but I represent her family."

"I can tell you what I can tell the family. We're working on it. We've interviewed anyone here who knew her. But she disappeared in Tulsa, and that's outside our jurisdiction."

"And... after six months... you're no longer working hard on it, are you? You can't be. I looked up the Lupiti PD online. You're one of two officers, plus the chief. Three people to handle this city, plus all tribal members. You can't have much time at all to give to a gone-cold disappearance from outside your jurisdiction."

He just stared at me.

"I'm new to this P.I. business. This is only my second client. I'm going to get this same wall of nothing from the Tulsa PD and the FBI, aren't I?"

His mouth twitched. "Don't forget the county Sheriff."

I smiled big, not meaning it, and nodded. "And the county Sheriff."

We looked at each other. I had to at least try.

"I'm a new P.I., but I'm not new at finding people. In fact, I'm good at it. I've looked for eight people in the last three years and found them all. They weren't all alive when I found them, but I found them."

I looked at him. He was at least listening. "I don't expect that will make any difference with the Tulsa PD, or the FBI or the Sheriff. They're big bureaucracies, and they represent tens of thousands — even millions — of people.

"But you and the Lupiti police... The Stintsons live in your town. You probably know the parents personally?"

He nodded slowly.

"You may even know Alaska personally. And her kids."

His eyes had gone unfocused.

"Do *you* think she ran away with a boyfriend?"

He shook his head no. "She wouldn't."

"I've got a genius computer tech and myself — we're devoting 100% of our time to finding her. It's your best chance for a break in the case. You know that."

Slowly, as though it was being dragged out of him, he said, "If you find someone who's hurt her...."

He was worried I'd act like a vigilante. I told him, "I would not do anything that would prevent that someone from facing justice."

I could honestly say that — because if the law didn't bring justice to such a man, I would. Instead, I asked, "Have you got any outstanding questions you wanted answers to? Anything or anyone you'd like researched?"

"One thing," he said. "It may not be related. Eleven months before Alaska, an Osage woman went missing from the same casino. She was also an employee — a maid. Her name was Alissa Barnett."

"Thank you. I'll look into her."

We sat there. I could see he was considering something, so I kept my mouth shut.

Finally, he said, "Your computer guy is really good?"

"A genius."

"Don't make me regret this...."

"Her parents will thank you."

"Alaska had an enemy. A guy named Colby Wyatt. He's a Class 3 registered Sex Offender. She saw him talking to her daughter Macey a couple of years ago. She got the town so riled up against him, he had to move out of his mom's house in town. He's now living in a trailer just outside the city limits."

"Class 3 in Oklahoma covers a lot of ground. What'd he do?"

"Look it up. Just don't go visit him alone. You're too old for his tastes, but he's mean as a snake. He could make an exception for you."

"Thank you."

I left with two more names for Mason to work on.

7

Mason Spencer
Lupiti, Oklahoma

Mason hated this.

His partnership with Sara was built on *her* doing all the people work — not him. His job was to sit in his comfortable lair and steal people's secrets. With his computers. With his food, drink, and equipment all exactly where he wanted it. Wearing anything he felt like — or nothing at all. With nobody there he had to make nice with.

He should be digging up more info on that liquor store guy, Joe Bob Morton. Whatever the cops had done about him three years ago hadn't made the newspapers. The guy didn't have a police record of any kind. He needed to put the guy under a microscope. People connections. Money. Emails if he could find them.

He'd already looked into Alaska's ex-husband, who should have been an excellent suspect. Unfortunately, Willie Brown was on camera going into an Oklahoma City bar 10 minutes before Alaska disappeared. That didn't prove he was innocent, however. Mason should be looking into his bank accounts right now.

Instead, he was here. He'd been here four days now, and he was getting more and more antsy. He needed to get back home and away from all this social stuff.

This afternoon had been excruciating, and it wasn't over yet. Some of Alaska's friends and neighbors were Lupiti. Mason agreed it made sense for him to join Sara in those visits — with him there, they were more likely to get answers.

Already they'd visited with two of Alaska's Lupiti neighbors. They had to greet each. Come in. Take tea or coffee. Discuss the weather. Smile.

Mason rubbed his mouth with his hand. His face hurt from smiling all afternoon. Computers didn't force you to smile. You didn't have to surreptitiously stare at computers to see if they were lying to you. You didn't have the responsibility of figuring out if a computer murdered someone.

A heavy-set woman with a turquoise necklace and red eyes — as though she'd been crying — opened the door.

"Naawaa." He greeted her with a smile. "Are you Jane Evans?"

She nodded.

"I'm Mason Spencer, son of Carol Red Eagle. This is Sara Flores. We're helping the Stintsons find their daughter Alaska."

Jane just stood there.

"Is this a bad time?" he asked.

She shook her head and waved her hand at her eyes. "My allergies are strong today. Come in."

They entered a small living room with two sofas, both covered with Native blankets. Kid toys were on the floor. Mason and Sara sat while Jane went to the kitchen to make coffee.

She brought out a tray with three mugs on it. Sara sipped hers and said, "It's very good." Mason sipped his and nodded. Both of them hated coffee, preferring their caffeine in soft drinks instead.

"It's Spirit Mountain's MMIP brew," Jane said. "Even though Alaska is white, I still think of her when I drink it."

She stared at Sara.

Sara recognized the challenge. Thanks to Judy's briefing, she wasn't ignorant. She asked, "Is it similar to MMIW?"

Jane broke her stare. "Yes. It's for 'people' instead of only 'women.'"

She turned and looked at Mason. "I met your mother at the Homecoming Powwow. You must be the one they call Huhatawuh Kíta."

Mason nodded. He saw Sara look at him. "It means digger."

Sara smiled and nodded.

"Why are you here?" Jane asked, looking at Sara.

"We were hoping you could tell us about Alaska. Her mother says you're her best friend."

"I was. Not so much since she got the job in Tulsa. It changed her."

"How?"

"She got too busy. She lost interest in the people here. She was always in Tulsa. Or taking her son to see that college in Los Angeles."

"How was she in the weeks before she disappeared?"

Jane's mouth twisted. "All she could talk about was wanting to get promoted in her job. To 'cage manager.' Do you know she worked in a cage?"

"She was a cashier, right?"

"They put them in glass cages, like an animal. I went there once to see her."

Jane looked at her watch. "I'm sorry," she said, standing up, "but I have to go pick up my children. Is that all you need?"

Mason stood up, and Sara joined him. "It's good for now," he said. "Although I hope we can contact you if any new questions arise?"

"Of course."

Jane saw them to the door. As they were leaving, she said, "Have you talked to her boyfriend?"

"Boyfriend?"

"I don't know who it is, but I know she had one. It had to be someone from her job because I'd know if it was someone from here."

Sara got in the passenger seat of Mason's rental car. He turned to talk, but Sara shook her head.

"Let's get some food and go to the office," she said, then turned away. Topic closed.

Mason frowned. He started the car and turned toward Tulsa. Sara was acting like the car might have been bugged. They'd been inside long enough for someone to have done it — but they would have to have planned it beforehand.

He smiled.

He was looking forward to figuring it out.

8

Sara Flores
Office building in Tulsa

I sat across from Mason in the office, watching him use chopsticks to stuff General Tso's chicken in his face.

He was smiling. His real smile, not the phony one he'd worn all day. Between mouthfuls, he was explaining how he'd checked the car for listening or tracking devices and how he was sure it was bug-free.

"What made you suspect a bug?" he asked.

"Something was off with Jane. Most people have to get to know me before they dislike me. But... I probably overreacted."

"No such thing in our business."

"Thank you," I said. "For coming along with me all day. And for being here for a record four days now. I know you hated it."

"Not re..." He broke off mid-sentence and stuck his chopsticks in the food container. He looked directly at me. "I hated every minute of it. But I can do more." He gulped. "I really want to help the Stintsons."

"You're sprung. I needed you for the Lupiti interviews, but not for the others."

The look of relief on his face was strong enough to make me feel guilty.

"Go home. I need you for the stuff only you can do. Find out more on that Joe Bob Morton. Any guy who owns a liquor store must have all sorts of illegal temptations. And get into Alaska's emails and see if you can find this boyfriend she supposedly had. I'll ask when I interview her work friends, but that'll be a couple more days.

"Also, run a genealogy DNA search for us. You have her parent's and her daughter's DNA samples. Let's make sure she isn't already in a database somewhere — like a morgue or hospital or prison."

Mason nodded. "That's next on my list." He got up and went to my mini-fridge and grabbed a can of Diet Mountain Dew.

I frowned. "How did that crap get in my fridge?"

Mason smiled.

"Judy? You had her stock that poison in my fridge?"

Mason shrugged. "Half is still yours. Half is mine. Only fair since we're partners.

He took a long swig from the can, then sat back down. He picked up the chopsticks again, grabbed the last piece of chicken, and popped it in his mouth.

"Nobody can eat that much and weigh as little as you do." I'd finished eating an hour ago. Mason was still going, scarfing down both the remains of my meal plus his own two servings.

He nodded, his brows furrowed, looking very concerned. "I'd heard old people have to eat less. It must be hard for you."

I gave him my worst "I'm going to kill you" stare.

Mason finished chewing and said, "I broke into the National Crime Information Center database already."

I grinned. "Of course you did."

"Perhaps Alaska was thought to be native when she was taken. I wanted to see what patterns I could find."

"And?"

"The databases don't list where the person was last seen, so I can't sort for casino disappearances."

"I hadn't thought of that. Casino disappearances in general — not just a disappearance from this one casino. Plus, native disappearances. Plus, non-native female disappearances. Plus personal motives."

Mason nodded. "Think we're in over our heads?"

"Probably," I said, smiling. "But when has that ever stopped us?"

9

Connor Rockwood
Four Leaf Clover Casino

Connor Rockwood knew how to size up people and situations quickly. Eleven years of body guarding CEO assholes had taught him that.

Like now.

He was seated in the small but luxe office of the Security Director for the Four Leaf Clover Casino. The man was slick with his expensive suit, shiny hair, and his trendy 2-day stubble. Appearances were important to George Moretti. As was being the top dog in the room.

George's handshake was too strong, like he had something to prove, and Connor had to fight the impulse to crush the man's knuckles. Just a little.

George had motioned Connor to a chair then sat himself down behind his desk, his nose in the air like he was a king who had granted an audience to one of his minions.

Connor carefully did not smile. He was used to dealing with men like this. Almost all his clients thought they were tough guys, just because they were able to "win" in business. And they figured they were superior to him because they were paying for his services.

This man would never agree to hire someone who might make him look bad. He wasn't getting inside here — unless he could make George look smart.

While body guarding CEOs, Connor had overheard a lot of negotiations. Time to put some of that to work.

Moretti said, "You've got an impressive resume, Mr. Rockwood. But I don't quite see what you could do for us in the two months you're available while your arm heals."

Connor leaned back in his seat and crossed his legs. "Well, sir, here's what I don't like about bodyguard work. You're mostly playing defense. Sure, you design your reaction plays; you anticipate. But mostly you're waiting for bad guys to make their moves. I think that might be a little bit like what you're forced to do in your job here.

"Occasionally, I get a really smart client who hires me to play offense. Who wants me to look at his operation as though I were the bad guy. See if I could get to the client. Museums and art galleries do it all the time."

Connor paused to let Moretti consider it.

"I think that might be a really smart way to test your setup here. A way to be proactive, not just reactive."

"Interesting," said Moretti, "but our security is state of the art. We move chips from tables to the cashier and back several times a day, and we've never had one attempt at theft."

Connor nodded. "I was thinking more of employee and customer security. Like your two employees that were taken from here, almost a year apart." He looked down at his notes. "An Alaska Brown and a Alissa Barnett."

George sat up straighter. "It hasn't been proved they were taken. One of them was reported leaving with a boyfriend, and the other might have been ducking out on one."

Connor raised an eyebrow.

"Besides, if they were failures, it was due to not having enough security cameras. Our Surveillance Director, Jerry Phillips — who handles electronic security — has since added over 50 additional cameras. I handle physical security."

"Surely they intersect a lot?"

George nodded. "We meet weekly. But you can rest assured that two vans in the parking lot won't be enough to hide anyone now."

Connor smiled. "And yet, that's the thing about bad guys, isn't it? They often find another way. Think how smart and forward-looking you'll appear to management if you set up a test."

George smiled back. "Think of how annoyed they'd be if I wasted the money to hire you and nothing was found."

Connor nodded. "You're right. So... how's about I help you with that. You hire me to proactively test employee and customer security — and you get me for free. Unless I find something, in which case you pay me $50,000. Which I'm sure management would welcome paying if it allows this place to plug a security hole."

George's eyes were unfocused, so Connor shut up and let him think. Finally, George nodded. "That might be interesting. We'd need a time limit. Thirty days?"

"Forty-five."

"Agreed. We'd need to pin down what constitutes a 'security hole.'"

"I can write up something on that. Get it to you for your approval."

George nodded and stood up. Connor stood as well.

George said, "I'll have to run it by the General Manager, but I'm pretty sure he'll go for it."

"I'll have a draft contract for you by tomorrow."

George came around the desk and shook hands. Again crushing harder than was polite.

As Connor turned to go, George said, "Thirty-five thousand, not $50,000. *If* you succeed."

"Forty-five."

"Forty."

"Agreed," said Connor. "I'll put that in the draft as well."

Connor looked around as he walked out of the casino, keeping a neutral expression on his face for all the cameras. He waited until he'd driven six blocks away until he let himself grin. He'd won everything he'd gone for. He was getting into the casino with a reason to hang out and look everywhere.

And, after the negotiating, he was getting $5,000 more than he expected. When he succeeded.

And he would succeed.

10

176 Days Earlier
Alaska Brown
Unknown Location

Alaska Brown woke up in yet another cell. The stench of sweat, blood, and paralyzing fear made her jerk up off the bare mattress her nose had been pressed against.

Too fast. She pressed her hands against the white concrete wall to steady herself from dizziness. Her stomach rebelled and she tasted acid in her mouth, along with something chemical. She had been drugged.

Again.

She looked for a place to throw up but saw only a small hole in the concrete floor with some brown smears surrounding it. Quickly she looked away and willed herself not to throw up.

No, no, no, no, no! She swallowed more acid and wrapped her arms around her stomach, taking shallow breaths.

Slowly her stomach settled.

When the urge finally passed, she looked at her surroundings. White painted concrete everywhere, except for one wall with a brownish-red stain a little over five feet above the floor. About the height of a woman's head.

The disgusting mattress she'd been sleeping on was on a metal shelf attached to the wall on one side and on two steel legs on the other side.

This cell was much worse than the last one. She didn't want to think about what that might mean for her future. Or her lack of one.

After being snatched along with Brittany Rebane, they'd been moved from one van to another and driven all night. They must have been drugged because they woke up in a different van with drivers who spoke only Spanish and wouldn't answer any questions.

Another long drive, another drugging, and Alaska woke up alone in one cell, then in another.

The last cell before this one, there had been young women in nearby cells. They only lasted a few days before they were replaced by other young women. Alaska could hear them crying at night.

Men also came to visit the other women. Never for long — minutes only. They came like they were inspecting merchandise. Open one cell. Look it over carefully. Close the cell and move to the next.

Twice one of the visitors looked into the window in her door, but — with a glance — moved on. No need to open her cell for a closer inspection.

For which Alaska thanked God most fervently.

She was jolted back to the here and now when the door of her newest cell opened.

A man stood in the doorway. He looked almost a foot taller than her 5' 5" and had funny hair. It was receding badly, so he'd buzz cut what was left. It was about the same length as the beard stubble — so he looked like his entire head was covered in a shawl of stubble that covered everything except the front of his face, from his eyes to the top of his balding dome.

But his most eye-compelling features were arms sticking out of his t-shirt, which were as big as her thighs and covered in tattoos.

Also noticeable was the huge serrated knife he was using to clean under his fingernails.

Alaska shuddered.

"Miss Brenda will see you now," he said.

Alaska looked down at her clothing. Her good blue suit and pink blouse were wrinkled, filthy, and undoubtedly stank. But if this Brenda was working with the kidnappers — then she would expect that.

Alaska nodded, and exited the door, the man behind her. She hoped to get some idea of where she was, but at the end of the hall were steps she was told to climb. They went up two long flights of concrete stairs surrounded by concrete walls. Nothing to show where they were.

A single door was at the top. Alaska was told to knock on it. She did, and she heard a lock click.

"Open it and go in," said the man. He followed her into the room, closing the door. Then he walked to the one other door in the room and exited. She remained in the room, facing a woman seated behind a fancy desk.

Alaska looked around. She'd become obsessively aware of locks and doors in the last two weeks, so her first thought was that the door lock where she'd just entered must operate on a remote control.

Her second thought was how to get out the other door. But the gunman was probably standing outside that one.

She noticed the opulence of the room. A light fixture of five huge round brass globes hung over a wood-slab desk on brass "X" legs. A similar brown wood credenza sat behind it in front of floor-to-ceiling gray drapes.

Behind the drapes — oh my goodness — was genuine sunlight. Alaska wanted to tear them open and feel the sun. It had been weeks since she'd seen it, and the need brought tears to her eyes. There was also a huge bookcase, tellingly empty of books except for some leather volumes probably bought by the pound for show.

She turned her gaze to the woman behind the desk, wondering why the guard hadn't stayed in the room. Also, wondering what would happen if she just ran for the second door.

The woman was passing for mid-40s, but she had that buffed, nipped, tucked, and polished look of rich women in their 50s. Shiny brown hair with gold highlights falling to her shoulders. Perfect makeup. She wore a turquoise and gold chunky necklace and matching earrings that probably cost more than Alaska's house.

"The guard's standing outside that door," said the woman, nodding toward the second door. Then she tapped something on her desk.

Alaska looked and saw the strangest gun she'd ever seen. It was black with yellow stripes on the handle and yellow all around a huge muzzle. It looked like it would fire inch-thick bullets. She frowned at it.

"It's a taser," said the woman. "In case you're dumb enough to think about harming me."

Alaska looked, but there were no chairs anywhere in the room except for the one the woman was sitting on.

"You owe me," said the woman. "I saved your life. Nobody else wanted you. If you make me regret it... I can always change my mind."

There was so much wrong in what the woman said that Alaska's head was reeling. She was surprised to hear herself ask, "Where am I?"

The woman spread her hands. "All you need to know is this is your new world. It's time you learned how to survive in it."

The woman stared at her. "Listen carefully."

11

Sara Flores
Trailer, outside of Lupiti, Oklahoma

I stopped my Ford F150 pickup at the turnoff to Colby Wyatt's place. Ahead, the gravel road I was on turned into a burnt red clay — which shone in the 75-degree April sunlight.

I could see the tip of his trailer about 300 yards down the road. A few scrub oak trees surrounded it — just tall enough to hide most of the place. The rest of the land between me and there was thigh-high weeds, mostly dead looking.

This was not prime real estate.

Oklahoma has the stupidest sex offender classification system I've seen. Class 3 — their worst classification — covers violent rapists and child molesters, along with 18-year-olds who have consenting sex with 17-year-olds. How hard would it be for them to add a Class 4 category and move all the dangerous offenders up to that?

Colby Wyatt was a Class 3, and he'd be one of the first I'd move to a Class 4. He was in the system for multiple counts of assault and for the forceable rape of a 12-year-old girl. For which he'd served 15 years and was now out on parole.

Mason had dug into the records and told me the eight acres and trailer were owned by Althea Wyatt, Colby's mom. She used to rent it out to supplement her tiny social security check, but Colby moved in two years ago and the rent deposits to her account stopped.

I double-checked that my Colt 1911 was snug in the corset holster right under my bra, along with two extra mags. My right ankle holster held my Ruger Max 9 — upgraded from the older LC9 version to include bigger magazines. The sheathe holding my Spyderco knife ran up my left ankle. I patted a pocket full of zip ties and a small roll of duct tape.

You'd think being a werewolf meant I didn't need all the hardware, but I know from experience that isn't true. One reason is that the transformation takes me a full 60 seconds, during which time I am completely helpless. Another is that if I transform in front of someone, I'd better be willing to kill him.

Or go into hiding for the rest of my life.

So, really, being a werewolf only gives me superior strength and heightened senses of smell and hearing. And one amazing fallback plan if everything else blows up in my face.

I put the truck in gear and drove up to Wyatt's trailer. There was a beat-up white van parked on the end, so I pulled up next to it.

A van. When every other male in the state of Oklahoma drives a pickup truck.

Guess it's kinda hard to abduct some young girl in a pickup truck. And, yes, I'm assuming his jail time didn't turn him into a reformed man. So sue me if I'm not being P.C.

The trailer looked like it would fall apart if you tried to move it. It was dirty white, with the tiny windows used on cheap houses to save on A/C and heating. There was a narrow path beside it, leading to the front door about one-third down its length.

As I walked to the door, I smelled dust, rust, at least one dead animal, and urine from a man who apparently enjoyed peeing outside.

I noticed my heart speed up and my lungs take in extra air. God help me — I love the adrenalin rush.

All my life, I had to avoid activities and places where a "bad man"

47

might hurt me. Now I didn't. It's like wearing a tight corset that constricts your ribs so you can hardly breathe. Then you throw it off.

The thrill was addicting.

But it didn't make me rash. I did not step up the two steps to his door, as I could see the door opened out. Instead, I reached over the small railing and knocked hard on the door. Twice.

Nothing happened, so I repeated it. Harder.

"Go away," a deep, slightly slurred voice shouted.

"No."

I flattened my back to the trailer wall, between the door and a window. Light shifted to my left. He must have opened the curtains to look out.

The light shifted back. There was silence.

The door opened fast, slamming back against the trailer. Wyatt stood there at the threshold and glared at me. He looked just like his booking picture. Brown, matted hair, brown eyes, and a brown mustache/goatee circle around his mouth. He was two or three inches taller than my 5' 7". He wore a dirty tee and jeans, the latter sagging on non-existent hips.

"Whadda mean no?"

"No. I'm here to talk to you."

"Tough shit." He reached for the doorknob to pull the door closed.

I held it open.

He frowned and jerked harder.

I didn't let it move. "Mr. Wyatt, I'm a private investigator looking into the disappearance of Alaska Brown. I have a few questions for you."

He must have realized he looked silly, pulling on a door that he couldn't move — so he gave up trying to close it.

"You and what army?" he asked.

"Just me."

"This here's private property. I'd be within my rights to shoot you."

From the moment he opened the door, I'd been inhaling through my nose, using my biggest superpower. Thus far, I'd smelled unwashed male and house stink, bologna and peanut butter — yuck combination! — and enough marijuana to give me the munchies.

I sniffed again. Guns are harder. If you haven't cleaned and oiled one in ages, I can miss it.

I didn't smell a gun, but I did smell... really?

My fists clenched.

I fake smiled. "I don't think you're stupid enough to have a gun. It's your fastest trip back to the joint. And you're not calling the cops. They'd get one whiff of the marijuana smoke in there and, again, back to the joint. Unless you have a medical marijuana license?"

He just stood there. Now I could smell fear on him. He was scared about something.

"Guess you don't."

I shrugged my shoulders. "Might as well invite me in. The sooner we talk, the sooner I'm gone."

He came quickly down the steps toward me. I let go of the door, and he slammed it shut behind him. He didn't want me in the house. Of course not. Not with what else I'd smelled.

"We can talk out here." He motioned toward the one folding lawn chair sitting with its back to the trailer. "Have a seat."

"I'll stand."

He leaned his back against the trailer. He pulled cigarettes from his shirt pocket and lit one up.

"Well?" he said, not looking at me.

"So far, I've found only two people who hated Alaska. You're one of them. That makes you a prime suspect."

He shook his head. "If I killed everyone I hated, there'd be a pile of bodies stacked up."

"You're saying she's been killed?" I inhaled deeply — getting all the scent from him I could. Surprisingly, the stink of fear was lessening. Talking about Alaska made him *less* afraid.

He sneered. "Women like her don't go missing willingly. Leave her kids? She's gotta be dead."

"Where were you on the night of Tuesday, September 17 of last year."

He gave me a look.

"Of course you know. You had to give the cops a good answer, or you'd have been their number one suspect."

"I was shooting pool down in OKC. Until 2 AM."

"Who do you think took her?"

"Don't know and don't really give a damn. Enough? Now leave me alone. And don't come back." His voice said he *really* didn't want me to come back.

So I wouldn't. No time like the present.

"I'll leave right after you introduce me to the woman you have in your trailer."

He stood up straight, his body vibrating with energy. "The hell I will."

"I don't think it's Alaska, but I want to verify. You show me an adult woman with no bruises on her, and I'm gone."

He looked at me. Then he let the tension gradually ease away, like air out of a balloon. He shrugged his shoulders and smiled.

"Sure." He mock bowed and swept his hand toward the trailer door. "Go on in and get your look."

I smiled back. "Thank you."

I stepped up the stairs and opened the door. He let me go all the way inside, following me. I walked into a living room and kitchen combination. Surprisingly clean.

There were no five-day-old fast-food wrappers lying around as I expected. Guess I'm prejudiced about the personal habits of scumbags. The only open food was a half-eaten peanut butter and bologna sandwich. On a paper plate.

I heard him close the door. I watched him, behind me, in the window glass, worried he'd have a knife. I didn't think he'd leave one lying around where a woman could get it, but I wasn't sure.

There was a slight scrape, and his hand came flying at my head from the side. Holding something in it.

I ducked really low, planning a fist to his genitals, but his swing turned him sideways. I almost punched the side of his exposed knee. It would collapse him, but probably break my knuckles.

Again.

No thank you.

Instead I put both hands on the floor and used my foot to smash the back of that knee. He flew forward, crashing onto a coffee table, his hands protecting his face.

He rolled to his back, reached into his boot, and came up with a switchblade.

He started to stand.

I took a quick step forward and kicked my cowboy boot right up under his chin, snapping his head back.

He collapsed back to the floor, and I moved quickly. I flipped his body over on his stomach, jerked his arms behind him, grabbed a zip tie, and fastened his hands. The knife was nearby, so I kicked it under the sofa.

I used my boot to push him over on his back, then pressed the boot into his stomach so he couldn't get up. Then I pulled out two more zip ties and connected them together.

He woke up, saw me, and started struggling.

I pulled out my Colt 1911 and pointed it at him. It's a big gun that looks even bigger when you're three feet from it and looking down the barrel.

There was a noise behind me, and I whirled. A face was sticking out from behind a door that led to what had to be a bedroom. The girl had a red and purple bruise covering the left side of her pale white face. Her eyes showed a full circle of white — they were open so big.

"Hi there," I said. "Show me your hands, sweetie."

Her face didn't move. No hands came out.

"Stick your hands around the door, please. Just let me see them."

Slowly two empty hands moved into view.

"Thank you. How old are you?"

Wyatt said, "She's 18."

The girl nodded slowly. "I'm 18."

I turned and kicked his ribs carefully — just hard enough to break a couple. I grabbed a towel from the kitchen, crammed it into his mouth and slapped some duct tape on to keep in the towel. Then I zip-tied his ankles.

Slowly I walked toward the bedroom door.

"My name's Sara. What's yours?"

"Candy."

"Hi, Candy. Can I come in?"

She nodded and backed away from the door. I saw she was short and dressed only in a thin tank-style undershirt and a pair of panties. There were more bruises on her arms — some purple and some a faint yellow.

"You want to sit down?"

She nodded, then ran into the closet and sat down inside, her back against a wall, her knees held up to her face. She carefully did not look at the bed.

I sat on the floor opposite her. "He can't hear you now, and I won't tell him what you say. I know you're not 18, but you're not in any trouble. How old are you really?"

She didn't look at me. "I'm almost 12."

I nodded and pulled out my phone. "I'm going to get you some help. And make sure that piece of garbage out there never bothers you again."

Judy was the first person I called, after swearing at myself for getting too dependent on her.

I asked, "Are there some kind of advocates in Oklahoma who can help an abused minor? I'm about to call in the cops, and I'd like someone here to help guide her through the process. To look out for her."

I gave her the address, and Judy said she'd get someone out here quickly. I knew if she said it, it was as good as done.

Then I called Sergeant Walker of the Lupiti PD and told him I just made a citizen's arrest and gave him the details.

Then I leaned back against the wall and knew I'd be answering questions in a dingy cop conference room for the next several hours.

And I was exactly nowhere on finding Alaska.

12

Connor Rockwood
Four Leaf Clover Casino

Connor pushed his empty plate away and leaned back in his chair. The steak was excellent, and, as promised, there wasn't a single disgusting pea in his vegetable mix. He shuddered at just the thought of the moldy cardboard taste of peas. Why anybody would….

Ah, well.

He smiled up at the two easily visible cameras watching this part of the restaurant. He suspected the casino Surveillance Director — Jerry Phillips — would have cameras following him wherever he went for at least the next two weeks. Maybe the entire 45 days of this assignment. There was something in his eyes when Moretti introduced him and explained Connor would be looking for physical security holes in the operation. Part of the look was competitive — he'd be happy if Connor found holes in Moretti's operation. But there was more there. Some kind of suspicion.

Connor had picked one of the restaurant tables close to the glass banisters that looked out and down onto the slot machine section of the casino floor.

He'd already decided he wouldn't pick a target from anywhere on that floor. Too many managers and plain clothes security walking around down there. No, he'd pick a target on the restaurant and shop floor. Or maybe in a hotel room.

The contract said he had to show he could commit first-degree burglary or first-degree robbery — both required threat to a person and taking $10,000 plus — and get away with it.

He'd asked Judy for a lawyer, and she'd found him a good one. The legal document he'd made them sign was 10 pages long and designed to be both iron-clad about the money they'd have to pay him and to keep him out of prison. As the lawyer explained, first-degree robbery in Oklahoma would get you five years to life — even if you used a toy gun. So he needed the protection.

He also knew how he'd get away with it. All the cameras made the casino overly confident. He'd have to make his face different enough to fool facial recognition. The cameras would see him, but they wouldn't recognize him. If they couldn't recognize him, they couldn't pin it on him.

He'd spend a few hours today and the next couple of days walking around the place. Looking. Checking out how vigilant each employee was. And getting them used to seeing him. His walk. How he dressed. How he looked.

Because when he made his move, none of those would be the same.

Four hours later, Connor drove home.

He'd become concerned.

In Special Forces, you depend on your sense of danger. He'd learned the hard way to trust it. If something made you uneasy, you damn well needed to be uneasy.

Connor was uneasy.

He stopped at a local drugstore, not one of the chains, and bought three burner phones. Then he called Sara on one of them.

"How fast can I meet you?"

"I'm at the office. You nearby?"

"I'll be there in 15. Don't let Judy go in any buildings until we talk."

13

Judy Street
Office building in Tulsa

Judy Street liked variety in both her men and her work, and she was getting it in this private investigator gig.

In one week, she'd had to find a great orthopedic surgeon, dig up data on missing persons, make travel arrangements, find a lawyer and a PTSD counselor, and learn how to gamble. And she'd met three handsome new men.

Today she'd been told to show up with a few of her bras and some way to hide a dime-sized transmitter on them. She'd stopped at JOANN's on East 71st Street and picked up some pretty flower appliqués that were either black or nude — the same colors as the bras she was bringing in.

She smiled. *Wouldn't it be wonderful if I finally found a job that won't bore me senseless after a few months?*

She walked up the flights to the office and winced yet again at the plain numbers on the door. There was no lettering with a professional-sounding name. The inside was even worse. Cheap chairs and a coffee table that looked like it was picked up at a dump. Plain table for a desk. And a rack of clothes on wheels. Like this was some kind of backstage dressing room.

She couldn't figure out this Sara Flores just yet.

The woman didn't like her, that was plain. Didn't want to work with her. And, yet, she kept hiring her? Most importantly, the woman didn't micro-manage her. She gave her a job and just assumed it would be done — and done well.

Judy was very tired of employers who treated her like an idiot when she could do the job better than they could.

Sara had to be smart — she'd apparently made a boatload of money finding people. But she seemed to have no idea how business worked. You had to look professional in business, or nobody would believe you were.

"Perception is reality" was Judy's buzzword. Maybe once they found Alaska, she could talk Sara into letting her set up the office so it looked better.

She'd talk to that cutie Mason first. He'd understand, and he could help her make Sara see the light.

Inside, she gave Connor a hug — the man was just a big teddy bear —and nodded at Sara. She pulled out the appliqués she'd bought and the only three bras she had with enough material to hold them.

"Will these work?"

Connor pulled out two discs which were the circumference of a dime but were thicker.

"Panic buttons," Connor said. "Half the size of those publicly available. Push one of these, and a text goes out to me, Sara and Mason. Along with the GPS of where you are. If you're being moved, you push it again to let us follow you."

Sara said, "Try not to push it when somebody can see you. You don't want them to know it's there."

Connor: "Women usually hide these in jewelry — earrings or a pin — but those get removed. I reckon this is more likely to stay with you."

Sara: "Wear it tonight, and I want you to promise to keep wearing it from now on. At home. Going to the grocery store. Keep wearing it until we say you can stop."

Judy looked between the two. She pulled up a chair and sat down. "Y'all'd best tell me why you think I need this."

Sara looked at Connor.

He nodded. "There's no intel that says you're at risk. Hundreds of thousands of women have been in that casino in the past year with nothing happening. Plus, you don't fit the target profile of the two that did."

"But..." Sara added. "You'll be asking questions."

"And..." said Connor, "something is off there. It's just a sense I got. But that sense has kept me alive. I trust it."

Sara: "You don't have to do this. I almost don't want you to. Doing this is *not* a requirement of your job. Nobody will think less of you."

Judy said, "So what you want is... I just go in, drink, eat, gamble — and chat up the employees. Like I'm idly thinking about working there? I just wear this panic button from now on."

Sara nodded, then turned to Connor. "I really think if there is a danger, it's more likely to be after she leaves the casino. Do you agree?

"More likely," Connor agreed. "But there's still danger at the casino. Keep aware."

Judy shook her head. "The chance of me happening to chat up our bad guy are ridiculously low... oh, I see. I'm to be bait. Stir things up. See who it upsets."

"Exactly," said Sara. "That's why I don't want you to do it unless you keep one of these buttons on you at all times. *All* the time. At home. Even sleeping."

Judy grinned. "As long as I don't have to wear one in the shower, I'll do it. Just let me sew these on, and then you can show me how they work."

Four hours later, Judy was at the casino.

At first, she was hyperaware of her bra, afraid she'd push it accidentally. But that fear eased. After all, how often did a woman push her breastbone right between her boobs?

Never — it turns out.

Unlike her last visit, Judy found herself obsessed with the

cameras in the place. Knowing they watched her every move was just creepy. She pictured some guy tracking her. Who better to disappear women than a guy who could track her every move. She shivered.

Judy stopped first at Georgio's Grille in the casino. She was able to sit at a counter with other singles — she now hated restaurants without that option. She had a delicious grilled steak salad with creamy tiramisu for dessert.

Sandy was the counter waitress and Judy confided in her that she was thinking about getting back to a waitress job now that her youngest was in college.

"I never thought about doin' it at a casino. Are the tips better?"

Sandy looked around to see who else was in earshot. "Tips are about the same — with an occasional big one from a winner. But your base pay is $2.15 an hour."

Judy's jaw dropped. "That can't be true, girl. What about minimum wage?"

Sandy shook her head. "They say it's legal because we get tips."

A diner at the end of the counter said, "Miss," and Sandy moved away to serve him.

Judy added a $50 tip to her check — she felt bad for the woman. *What would her weekly paycheck look like? $2.15 times 40 hours would be, what? $86? I can't believe it!*

Another benefit to her leaving a $50 tip would be seeing how Sara would react. Judy had no idea what Sara would do when she saw it, and she wanted to know. It was annoying not to have a better read on the woman.

Judy spent an hour playing different slot machines and lost $150. The cocktail waitress who brought her a drink wasn't forthcoming about her job. To her question of, "Is this a good place to work?" she was told, "Sure," and the woman took off immediately to look for another customer to serve.

She spent another hour losing $300 in poker. The waitress there put on a big phony smile and told her it was a wonderful place to work.

Seeking a better place to strike up a conversation, she went to the poshest-looking bar, with a handsome man tending it, and ordered a Glenfiddich on the rocks.

Judy took a sip and sighed. "Honey, can I ask you a question?"

The man smiled. "Sure."

"I just lost $450 in two hours. Is that normal, or do I suck at gambling?"

He smiled. "I had a man here once tell me he dropped $50,000 in one hand of baccarat. So I think you're a long way from sucking."

Judy crinkled her brow. "You know, it's not as much fun as I thought it'd be. I've played poker and the slots. Is there something else I should try?"

He cocked his head. "Have you tried the craps tables? People there get the most excited."

Judy smiled. "Thanks, hon. I might just try that."

The man moved over to serve someone else.

When he came back, she said, "I'm fixin' to get a job now that my kid's in school. I did some bartending previously. Some waitressing. Do you recommend this place?"

His smile disappeared, but then he brought it back. "Sure. It's a great place. But you'd have to be willing to work from 10 at night to six in the morning. All new people start on that shift."

"Ooh, I don't know. I'll have to think about that."

Judy called her private car service. When they texted her, she left $30 on the counter, double what she owed, and left.

Once in the car, she took a huge breath and noticed her hands were shaking. She had been frightened. She traced her exit in her mind and realized there were two very good-looking men she'd passed, and she hadn't even smiled at them.

Between the exit and the camera eyes on her....

Being bait was exhilarating, but maybe it was a thrill best experienced just once.

14

Judy Street
Home in her apartment

Judy woke up in the middle of the night with a heavy weight pressing down on her chest. She opened her eyes — only to see jade-green eyes staring at her from just inches away. It was her bi-colored Persian cat.

What the heck was wrong with Lola?

A quick glance assured her she was in her own bed. The pink and gray wall in front of her proved it. She'd had to get permission from the landlord for the custom paint job, but it was gorgeous and well worth the hassle.

She was about to push Lola off her when she heard a soft scraping sound. It was the noise made by the sliding glass door to her balcony — she kept meaning to lubricate it but somehow never did.

Someone was coming in from her third-floor balcony.

Oh dang it!

Judy felt for the panic button, but she'd taken off the bra to sleep. She grabbed Lola and put her under the bed, then reached the chair with her bra and pushed the panic button.

Sure, she thought. *That'll work if I'm still alive in the half an hour before Connor can get here.*

Gun! Judy had forgotten she had one. She hadn't fired it in at least 10 years, but she had one. It was in the night stand.

Oh dang it! It was in the *other* nightstand. On the side of the bed by the door. Judy jumped on the bed and scrambled to the other side. She grabbed the drawer and pulled it out so fast it slammed into her leg.

Ow!

Judy grabbed the small handgun an old boyfriend had bought her and hoped to heck it would fire. She remembered him —Jim was his name — warning her not to leave a clip in because the springs might go.

Would they still work after 10 years?

She turned toward the bedroom door as a man in a black ski mask and black everything else — he looked like the night incarnate — came into the room.

Her finger jerked on the trigger as her hand came around, sending a bullet out wide.

He moved so fast. His gloved hands grabbed the gun and twisted it, breaking her index finger as he took control.

Judy screamed.

He cut off the scream, lifting her up and slapping his hand over her mouth, pulling her back tight against him. His other arm came around, catching her neck in the "V" of his elbow. Tightening it until she couldn't breathe.

For only the second time in her life, Judy swore. Right before everything went black.

15

Sara Flores
Outside Judy's apartment

I sat in my F-150 truck, parked half a block from Judy's apartment building. She was on the top floor of the three stories, facing the street, with a small recessed balcony you couldn't even see because she'd loaded the railing with a couple hundred flower pots.

The lights in her apartment were off.

I knew watching her place was ridiculous, but I was just paranoid enough to insist. I've spent two years worrying about Mason being hurt because of his association with me. I either work alone, or I'm going to worry. And take steps to ease that worry.

Connor and I were covering her for at least the first two nights. He took tonight's 7:30 - 12:30 shift, and all was clear. I'd relieved him just an hour ago.

A smile crossed my face as I pictured him at home now with Lillian — a former client of mine. They were perfect together. She understood the military — she'd lost a foot driving a truck in Operation Iraqi Freedom. But she softened his hard edges. Just a little.

I pulled a Diet Coke out of my mini cooler on the passenger floor, then unwrapped my favorite treat in the world — a caramel-covered marshmallow. I plopped the entire thing in my mouth and swooned. Oh, the taste of the caramel as it starts to melt in the heat of your mouth. Oh, the squishy goodness of marshmallows.

I closed my eyes in delight.

When I opened them, I saw a black, beat-up Chevy cargo van with a small corporate sign on the side. Something Electronics — I couldn't catch the first part.

Better eyesight is *not* one of my gifts from my wolf. Just the opposite — I think my vision is worse than it was before my transformation. I grabbed my binoculars from the seat.

The van drove past the apartment and turned the corner. It was the first commercial vehicle I'd seen since I got here. I opened my notes app and spoke the license plate number. Then I called Mason.

It was 2:30 AM in his time zone — the middle of the work day for Mason.

"You bored?" I asked. "Want to look up a license plate for me?" I gave him the number.

I watched while I waited — half expecting the van to reappear.

"Got it. A white 2011 Nissan Urvan registered to Gary's Dry Cleaners."

My eyebrows went up. "An Urvan?"

Mason texted me a picture of a van with windows all along both sides.

"And yet that license plate is now on an electronics company's Chevy van."

"Somebody took the bait?"

I winced at Judy being bait. But...

"Can you get a visual on the van?" I asked Mason. I knew he could hack into the huge Tulsa camera system that spied day and night on all of us Tulsans.

I told him, "It drove east on Hudson about five minutes ago and turned right on Beech. I'm going to go inside."

I patted my guns, knife, and zip ties, then put my phone in my vest pocket, leaving the connection with Mason open.

I put my hand on the lever to open the car, then froze. A black man-shape had come around the side of the building. He stood there for a minute, looking up. Then he stood on a railing surrounding the patio of a ground-floor apartment and reached up. Quickly he was on the second-floor balcony.

Before I could react, he was reaching for the third floor and Judy's balcony.

As he climbed over her railing, I jumped out of my truck and ran across the street. I heard the smashing of a flower pot.

The fastest way to Judy was to follow him up. I figured if he could do it then so could I. However, he was taller than me, so I twice had to jump to reach the next level.

I was grateful for the extra leg muscle I had.

Halfway up I heard a gunshot.

"*Merde*." It was my late mother's favorite word for trouble.

Mason's voice came out of my vest pocket. "What's happening? Should I call someone?"

"Gunshot," I said. "Call an ambulance only. And shut up, I'm going in."

I climbed over the railing — over the one spot that didn't have a plant on it, because the pot was lying smashed on the balcony.

Mason had sent Connor and me the floor plan for Judy's apartment when we decided to post a watch. I'd thought it was overkill. Now I was grateful. The sliding glass door led into the living room. Directly across it was an open door that I knew led to her bedroom.

I hurried through the sliding door just as a black-clad man came out of the bedroom door, carrying Judy, and turning toward where the apartment door was.

He saw me a split second after I saw him. I leapt into the air to reach him, flying the 12 feet and barreling into them.

The three of us hit the wall and slid down. He let go of Judy and got both hands around my neck. I didn't fight his grip but reached down my left leg and got my Spyderco knife.

His chest was padded — he was wearing Kevlar. Odds were good it was Kevlar that protected from bullets but not from edged or spiked weapons, but I wasn't going to risk it. I raised the knife between us and stabbed him in the throat, then jerked the blade to the side, severing jugular veins and his windpipe.

Blood sprayed out over me as his hands let go of my neck and moved to his own. He fell away.

I moved quickly to Judy's side. She was breathing and had a pulse. She was sound asleep, despite falling to the floor.

"Mason," I said. "The man's dead. Judy may have been drugged. ETA for the ambulance?"

"Two minutes. Call the cops?"

"I'll do it. Keep you out of it." I ripped off the dead guy's ski mask and didn't recognize the man. I sent his picture to Mason.

Then I looked at Judy. He'd been carrying her out of the building.

"Mason, he had to have a partner. Maybe outside right now. I'm going. Give the ambulance her apartment number. I'll prop the outside door open."

I ran outside into the hall, dialing 911. I gave them the address and said, "My client was drugged. Ambulance called. I killed her attacker. I'm running now to find if he had a partner. Will be back." I hung up.

I raced down the interior stairs and out the front, leaving a ball-point pen holding the door from latching.

Nobody was there.

I heard the sound of sirens coming and ran around the building on the side the man had used. I saw the battered black van and started for it.

Too late, I registered the man smell beside me. He'd been right around the corner.

What an idiot I was.

I dropped to the ground just as something whooshed over my head and clanged into the side of the building. A metal pipe?

Stupid. Stupid. Stupid. But I was just so *angry*. At myself — for putting Judy at risk like this.

His feet were right in front of me, so I grabbed his ankles and jerked. He landed on his butt, and I jumped on top of him. He was wearing Kevlar as well.

My wolf was sending me enticing pictures of biting his throat out, but I had just enough brains overriding my anger to realize that would be my stupidest move yet.

He was wearing the same thing as the other man, including the pull-down black mask with eye holes. Did they get matching outfits? Who dresses these guys?

His right fist slammed into my head, causing me to reconsider. Fashion shouldn't be my focus here.

He'd knocked me to the side, and my head hurt like a son-of-a-gun, but lying on his back meant he couldn't get much power behind the punch.

I noticed my knife was still in my right hand. I had a flash of desire to plunge it into him, like his partner, but instead I flipped my hand 180 degrees and slammed the hilt of the knife into his temple.

Twice.

Then I flipped him and zip-tied his hands and feet. I stood up and managed, with great difficulty, not to kick him.

I pulled his mask off and stared at him. I'd never seen him either. I snapped another picture and sent it to Mason.

Then I looked around and remembered the van. I ran to it and opened the doors. Nobody was inside. The back of the van was open, and the inside was... interesting. It had carpeted floors and welded eyebolts on the walls. Two pairs of handcuffs lay on the carpet.

How long before the cops would get to it? I pulled a gun and blew a hole in each of the four tires. But the vehicle only dropped down half of what it should. Run-flat tires?

I went back to the driver's side and flipped the hood latch. Then I opened the hood and put my remaining four bullets into what I thought was the radiator, carburetor, oil tank, and — standing back and squinting my eyes — some part of the engine. I was afraid that the bullet would ricochet, but it didn't.

I walked back to the zip-tied man and stood staring at him. Finally, I asked Mason, "How's Judy?"

"The ambulance is there now."

"Get Connor to the hospital to protect her. I'm going to be tied up with cops for god knows how long."

I could hear two new sirens coming closer.

I looked down at myself — bathed in blood. Oh boy. I'd be lucky not to be shot on sight.

"Mason? Hire me a really good criminal attorney. I'm sorry to put this on you. I should have asked Judy days ago to do this. We'll probably need one on retainer."

I shook my head. "This all seemed so easy two years ago. Now we're a fucking conglomerate."

I walked about 15 feet away from the now-awake-and-struggling man and put my knife and empty gun on the ground. I added my backup Ruger Max 9 from my right boot. Then I pulled out my P.I. badge in its case. From a distance, it looks like a cop badge. Maybe it would help — until they realized it wasn't one of theirs.

Holding both hands up, one empty and one with the badge, I moved until I could be seen from the front. Two cop cars slid to a halt in front of the building.

Four cops rushed out the doors to the sidewalk. One of them saw me, pointed his gun at me, and yelled for me to stop.

Three other guns quickly joined his in pointing at me. "Who are you?" one of them yelled.

Very careful not to move, I said, "I called you."

A gurney rolled down the sidewalk to the ambulance.

"That's my client. Two men tried to abduct her. One's dead upstairs. The other is alive back behind me. Please make sure you check out the van back here that they were driving. I shot it up so nobody could remove it. You'll see handcuffs in it."

"Your client?"

"I'm a P.I."

All four sets of lips curled in disgust.

"Whose blood is that on you?" asked one of them.

"It belongs to the man upstairs who attacked my client."

One of the cops moved toward me. As he got closer, he noticed my guns and knife on the ground behind me. "These weapons yours?"

"Yes," I said. "Two more things. You might want to contact Detective Alberto Rodriguez. He knows me. And, I've contacted an attorney. I won't say any more until after seeing him."

Now, of course, they really hated my guts. A private investigator *and* someone demanding an attorney. Two huge strikes against me.

16

Sara Flores
Tulsa PD interview room

I'd been sitting in the smelly, depressing precinct "interview room" for almost two hours, bored enough to start screaming. The chairs dug into my butt, the puke-green metal table was chipped, and the mirror — behind which cops could be staring at me — was burning a hole in the back of my head.

Not to mention how clammy the congealing blood all over the front of my clothes felt. It had started to stink two hours ago.

How do other P.I.'s stand the waiting around?

Robert B. Parker's Spenser says he runs through past Boston Red Sox games in his head. I love the New York Mets. Watch almost all their games. But I couldn't run through a single game from memory. That ability may be a guy-thing.

Jack Reacher runs through prime numbers in his head. Forget that, I barely know what a prime number is. Some fictional P.I. — I can't remember who — plays songs in his head. I couldn't do that without starting to belt out the song. Probably not a good idea in cop central.

You may think me an idiot for turning to fictional P.I.'s for tips, but I've never met any real ones.

I was about to go with the gold-standard boredom response of banging my head against the table when the door *finally* opened, and in walked the grizzled Detective Alberto Rodriguez and his young partner Jake Sloan.

The two of them were involved in my first P.I. case, two months ago, where a powerful local businessman tried hard to kill both my client and me. Rodriguez was smart — a negative for any cop I have to deal with — but at least he wasn't a power-mad asshole. I think he ended up okay with me. I was never connected to all the bodies that solved my case. And, besides, they were found outside his jurisdiction.

Rodriguez was small, wiry, and well past the age when he could retire from the force with full benefits. Sloan was young, new, tall, and had Oklahoma farm boy written all over his freckled face.

"Sara Flores. Not surprised to be seeing you again." Rodriguez pulled out a chair and sat down. My ears could hear him crunching an antacid he must have popped into his mouth before coming into the room. I remembered he threw away the green ones, and I shook my head at the worthless stuff crammed into my brain.

"Nice outfit you got," said Sloan.

"Red's the new "in" color," I said. "Where's my attorney?"

"He's coming," said Rodriguez. "Some reason you need an attorney this time? You didn't ask for one the last time we talked."

"I was young and naive then."

"Two months ago?"

I sighed. "This P.I. business ages you quick. Sorry, Rodriguez. Nothing more until I talk to my attorney."

They both got up and left.

Fifteen minutes later, an attorney came in. He put a little kick in my blood pressure because his face and eyes looked like a young Alan Rickman. Except this man wore a goatee and slicked his hair down neat instead of sporting Rickman's mussed-bed-hair that so made you want to run your fingers through it.

Atticus Snowden — I knew the guy was costing me a fortune with that name — told me he'd been contacted by Mason Spencer, and we agreed he would represent me. I brought him up to speed. He had a good poker face, listening as though what I described was an ordinary night for a client.

Then we called Rodriguez and Sloan back in, and I gave my recorded statement, describing everything. I included Judy's involvement in the case, but I downplayed her trips to the casino. Atticus allowed me to answer questions clarifying what happened, but he shut me down when they tried to turn their interests more to me as a person.

Twice, when he stopped a question, he said, "You boys should be thanking my client for stepping up and being a good citizen. She took two obvious criminals off the street so they can't hurt any more taxpayers in this town."

Finally, when they started to ask the same questions for the third time, he said, "That's enough for tonight. My client needs a shower and some sleep. You have any more questions, you can call me in the morning."

Rodriguez and Sloan stood up.

"Wait a minute," I said. "I've got an employee still at risk. Can you tell me who these two guys were? I need to know who to protect her from."

The men looked at each other. Rodriguez nodded, and Sloan left the room. Rodriguez leaned his back against a wall.

"They're both known members of the Vipers," he told me.

I frowned at him.

"It's a local gang — started about six months ago, but growing fast. The leader is Dwayne Tyler — street name Adonis. They're into gun running, drugs and forgery. This is the first attempted kidnapping we know of."

"Thanks."

"Come in tomorrow and sign your statement."

"I will."

He was opening the door when I said, "Rodriguez?"

He looked back at me.

"If this is new for the gang — could they have been paid to do it for someone else?"

He looked at me. "It's something we're investigating."

Then he tilted his head to the side. "Flores, you stay away from Dwayne Tyler. You mess with my investigation, and I'll toss you in jail for obstruction."

Well, damn.

I was so tired it was almost stupid to drive myself home, but I did. I kept awake by calling Mason on the way to update him. I was almost home by the time I finished.

"Mason, I need you to take the lead on this one. Nobody else can do it. Write the book on this Dwayne Tyler, aka Adonis. But especially look for connections to someone bigger, more powerful, probably more respectable. Maybe he met them in his childhood or early years. But I want to know everything he said or did from the first moment Judy went into that casino. Who called him. Who he might have seen. Texts. Emails. Anything you can get that could tell us who might have hired him to go after Judy."

Mason was quiet, then said, "You know we might not be able to find something that subtle."

"I know it's probably impossible — which is why I'm depending on you to find it."

"Oh," he said. "Well, in that case..."

17

Mason Spencer
Lock Haven, PA

Mason woke up early for him — it was barely noon. He looked out the window of his home at the inch of snow still on the ground, even though the calendar had just turned to April.

He'd wanted so bad to be back here at home, but now it felt like he should be in Tulsa. It was ridiculous. There wasn't anything he could do there that he couldn't do right here.

But he felt cut off from the action. He'd loved that feeling a year ago when he'd bought this house — right after he and Sara had made a killing.

Well... Sara had killed. Mason had just stolen the murderer's $2 million he had hidden in the Caribbean nation of Nevis.

Overnight, Mason went from college-student broke to flush. He put most of his half into an anonymous scholarship program for Lupiti students. But he'd taken $129,000 to buy this small 2-story red-brick house. It had 2 bedrooms on the top floor, which he'd opened up into his Command Central and which he protected with top-of-the-line security. He'd spent more than the house price up there.

Downstairs it looked like a regular house — where he could get packages and act "normal" and see friends from college. Or his parents.

Last night he'd been on a roll — eliminating a number of possibilities for where Alaska might be. He'd run her DNA and coordinated with the DNA Doe Project. None of the unidentified bodies matched Alaska's DNA.

However, just 25% of all unidentified bodies get their DNA submitted. The rest of the bodies go to an incinerator after just 30 days.

The National Crime Information Center had nothing new, and Alaska had never even been entered in the NamUs database.

He'd also dug deep into Joe Bob Morton, the bar owner Alaska got in trouble. Joe Bob was supposedly working right at the time of her disappearance. But he wasn't. Mason found a speeding ticket issued to him 15 minutes after she disappeared. But the location for that ticket was 45 minutes away from the casino. So if he'd had anything to do with her missing — he wasn't there in person.

The only outstanding problem was this Adonis gangster. Somebody big was paying him for the attack on Judy — that was clear. The gang had never tried anything like that before. Finding out who paid was the problem. Mason wasn't optimistic. Gangsters were usually the last people to leave an electronic trail.

Last night all hell had broken loose at Judy's apartment. He was so thankful they'd been watching it. The next time Connor had a bad feeling about something — he was going to trust it.

He'd found Sara the best criminal attorney in Tulsa and sent Connor to the hospital where Judy was taken. Then he sat back to let the adrenalin levels in his blood ease back from red-alert status.

Now... total silence. He felt isolated. Like it was a *bad* thing, not a good thing. He was surprised he'd been able to sleep last night.

His phone rang. It was Connor.

"They're discharging Judy today," he said. "Where should we take her?"

Mason heard a woman's voice in the background, then Connor said, "Judy wants to speak to you."

Her voice came over the phone. "Do y'all have this kind of thing happen often? Where you need a place to keep someone safe?"

"It does happen," he admitted. Heck, it had happened in their last case.

"Maybe out of town would be better?"

"Maybe… wait a minute. Do you have your personal cell on you?"

"Yes."

"Give it to Connor. Tell him to take it out to his car and leave it there. And bring you one of the burner phones he has. Call me back on it after he's searched your room for bugs."

"Whoa! We're going all James Bond — I love it!" She hung up.

Mason smiled and shook his head.

Twenty minutes later, she called him back on a burner. Her first words were, "Y'all got an extra $2-3 thousand a month you could spend on a safe place?"

"We could…"

"Let me find you a gated apartment with good security. Luxury — so thugs would stick out like a turd in a punchbowl. You'd want a big city — at least 500,000 people. Max three hours drive from here but across state lines. Maybe Wichita?"

"Judy," Mason said. "We're talking about for tonight."

"Let me get on it right now. Worst case, we'll have it by tomorrow night. Either furnished, or you'll have to give me $50K to make it livable. I'm assuming you have a dummy corp to hide who the owner is?"

"Yes…"

"Give me the name to use. Later you can come out and add your security on top of what the building offers. But by tomorrow, you'll have an easy, safe place to hide a client or anyone who needs it. Like me.

"Oh…," she added. "It needs to accept pets."

"Um… why?"

"Well, don't be silly, hon, I'm not going anywhere without my cat Lola. Now say goodbye so I can get started."

"Wait! Let me talk to Connor."

"Call him on his phone, sweetie. I'll be burning up this one." Judy hung up.

Mason raised his eyebrows. He felt like he'd been hit with a bulldozer. A sweet, polite bulldozer, but still... He called Connor.

"What just happened?" Mason asked.

Connor laughed. "She looks so harmless. But it makes sense."

"It does. We could have used it on the last job with Lillian. It would have kept us out of that hotel."

"Good. Have fun telling Sara about all this."

"Oh, shit." Mason hung up.

18

Mason Spencer
Lock Haven PA

Mason called Sara on their secure phones.

"Just a second," she said. He could hear traffic noises.

"Okay, I pulled over. We can talk for about 30 minutes. Then I'm meeting with casino bigwigs and a cashier who worked with Alaska. I'm hoping one of them knows about the boyfriend Jane Evans told us she thought Alaska was seeing."

"I'm not sure he exists," Mason said. "I've looked through all her emails, and there was nothing there. If she had one, they never emailed each other. Which seems unlikely."

"I'll know more in a couple of hours. Anything else?"

"Well... yes. By tomorrow we'll have a safe house. Maybe in Wichita. Judy's taking care of it."

"What???"

It took a while, but Mason gave her the full details. Sara hadn't said a word while he explained.

"Well?" he said once he'd finished.

"It's a really good idea — one you and I would never have come up with. And it'll hide Judy for the next week or two. Keep her safe. Boy, we're going to miss her after this case."

"After this case, there's no reason to miss her. She's a valuable team member."

Mason heard a blaring of horns. "What's going on?"

"Oh, some idiot pulled right into traffic, cutting another guy off. Now that guy's giving him the horn and the finger. Don't be surprised if you hear gunshots next. I might have to duck down behind the engine block."

"Sara. We need Judy."

Sara sighed. "She's a woman who was drugged, and her finger was broken. She was going to be tortured for information about us. Why else do you think she was kidnapped?"

"She knows that. She's asked me to beef up her personal security. She's got Connor teaching her a couple of Special Forces moves to incapacitate someone. She's also got him agreeing to take her to a shooting range."

"No, Mason. Just no. I'm not going to be responsible for getting her killed."

"What about Connor?"

"Him either. In two months, he'll be back at his bodyguard job."

"Oh, sure. Like that'll be safe for him. Like he even *wants* safe. Not everybody does, you know."

Sara hung up.

19

Sara Flores
Four Leaf Clover Casino

It took a not-so-veiled threat to get me this appointment with Gene Alderman, the manager of the Four Leaf Clover casino. His bulldog of an assistant, by the name of Linda Sue Mayweather, first insisted he was too busy, then suggested I instead see their Public Relations director. I told her I was willing to be palmed off on underlings, but only after I got 15 minutes with Alderman.

When that still didn't work, I said, "Ms. Mayweather, the disappearance of two of your employees and the brutal attack last night on one of your customers have so far received very little coverage in the press. Nobody is asking — yet — if they're all connected to your casino. And nobody needs to be asking that — *if* I get 15 minutes with Mr. Alderman."

Dressing for the meeting with him was a pain in the behind. I'd thrown away all my office clothes when I got divorced and left my job. I refused to wear a monkey suit again, but a business jacket over a pants outfit or a dress is thankfully acceptable for women. I added more sedate stud earrings instead of the dangly sliver-feather ones I prefer. Heck, I even put on some makeup. And, fortunately, the shag haircut I prefer looks stylish, even when it's mussed and only been finger combed.

Casino managers, by definition, must be charming, and Gene Alderman was no different. I got a big smile and a warm handshake as though it was his idea to meet with me. The man had a tanned mostly-bald dome accented by two sides of close-cropped gray hair. His tie was knotted so high up it had to be choking him. He was just under six feet tall and slim enough to be running on a treadmill every day.

His smile was as real as a salesman's.

"What can I do for you?" he asked, sitting back behind his desk with me across from him. The desk was clear except for a computer and a football with a bunch of signatures on it. The plaque said Oklahoma University Sooners -- 2020 Bowl Champions.

"As I told your assistant, I'm searching for Alaska Brown. I'd like to see what your security people have gathered on her disappearance."

"We gave all that to the police."

"The police don't share with private investigators. Neither do they have anything to lose if I decide the only way to get the info I need is to make a big public stink about people disappearing from your casino. I don't want to do that. I doubt I'd get anything good from doing it. But I need to see those reports."

He was silent.

"Full disclosure — I also want to interview your Security Director and your Surveillance Director. And talk to any of the cashiers who were friends with Alaska."

I held my hands up, palms forward. "After that, I'm out of your hair."

We sat there for almost a minute. Looking at each other.

He said, "What did you tell my assistant about a customer being attacked?"

"My assistant came in here two nights in a row, asking a bunch of questions. The third night two gangbangers broke into her apartment, drugged her and tried to kidnap her. I downplayed her being here to the cops because there may be no connection. But I want to see the security footage of her time here. Just in case it shows somebody reacting."

Alderman made his decision, nodded and stood. "Linda Sue will get you set up with the three appointments you indicated."

We shook hands again.

I stopped at the door on my way out and turned back to him. "One more thing... my assistant knows next to nothing about our investigation. If someone wants answers, I'm the one they should be asking."

He raised an eyebrow but said nothing.

I left.

Two hours later, I was back to meet with George Moretti, the Security Director.

His office was unusually plush, and his clothes, manner and smile were slick. Appearances were important to George.

"Gene said to give you whatever you need," he said, offering me a folder. "Here's what we gave to the police — our investigation on Alaska's last day here."

I held the folder in my hands, waiting for more. When he just looked at me, I said, "And the file for Alissa Barnett. Your maid that disappeared earlier that year."

His smile tightened at the edges, then smoothed out. He picked up his phone and asked his assistant to copy the investigation file on Barnett and bring it in.

"It'll be a couple of minutes."

I paged through the file he'd given me — all four sheets that were in it. Plus, there were two time-date stamped still photos from two video cameras of the last time they caught Alaska and a young woman I now recognized as Brittany Rebane. Just before their images disappeared behind both of the two vans that blocked the camera views. And two other photos taken 52 seconds later — when the vans were gone, and Alaska's car was just sitting there. Without her or the other woman.

I closed the folder and waved it at Moretti. "This isn't the whole file. I need Alaska's full personnel file."

Moretti shook his head. "Sorry, but privacy laws...."

I removed a piece of paper from my briefcase and laid it on his desk. "A signed authorization from her parents for me to receive all the information you have on Alaska. Results from any tests you gave her. Personnel reviews. Disciplinary notes. Raises. Promotions. Warnings. Everything."

"Her parents are not her. The privacy laws..."

"Full cooperation, remember? This paper from her parents will protect your company — given her disappearance."

Moretti's smile had slowly disappeared. His fingers were tapping on the desk. He picked up the phone again and called the HR Director. He got some pushback, but "Alderman okayed it" and "I'll give you a copy of the parent's authorization" ended the conversation.

He turned back to me. "You'll have it in a few minutes. Would you like to wait out in the lounge for it..."

"Two more things," I said. "First, what do you — as a man with your security background — think happened to Alaska."

"Personally? I think she left with a boyfriend — wanted a different life. That's how Rebane described it."

"And if she didn't? If this was a kidnapping, how smart, how knowledgeable, were the kidnappers? To pull this off the way they did?"

He sat up straighter, and his fingers stopped tapping. He liked being asked his opinion.

"They didn't need insider knowledge if that's where you're going. They needed to know Alaska's schedule — which was easy. She had regular hours. And they needed to have found the security cameras and figured out they needed two vans to block them."

I nodded. "Last question. How do I contact Brittany Rebane?"

"You can't. She's apparently driving around Mexico with her boyfriend."

"For over a year?"

Moretti shrugged.

"You don't find it suspicious they both disappeared the same night?"

"Rebane didn't disappear. She told her boss she quit right before she left that night. Told him to donate her last check to a charity. Said she was going to have fun in Mexico with her boyfriend. Her cell phone GPS showed her near Guadalajara."

"Then how was she interviewed about Alaska?"

"The police called her phone. She said Alaska got into a van with a guy. She thought they were lovers. That's all she knew."

"Description of the guy?"

"She barely saw him. Thought he might be Hispanic."

"Again, how do I reach her?"

"Her phone went dead after a couple of weeks. Still in Guadalajara."

"Family?"

"A mother who said 'Good riddance.'"

I rose to go. At the door, I turned. "These pictures of Brittany. She's an extraordinarily pretty girl."

"That's not illegal, last time I checked."

"No, but so was Alissa Barnett. It's a risk factor."

20

Sara Flores
Four Leaf Clover Casino

I don't know what I was expecting from the casino's Surveillance Director, Jerry Phillips. Certainly not what I got.

The man who stood up from his desk and came to shake hands had short, brown, receding hair, even though he couldn't be older than his mid-30s. He was sporting a geek-guy look with a button-down shirt collar although there was no pen protector. A suit jacket hung behind the door. His face was as white as a vampire's. Not surprising, I guess, when he spent all his time looking through cameras.

Adding up what Connor reported to me about locations, Phillips commanded an army of more than 600 cameras.

But that wasn't the big surprise — it came the minute the Phillips got close enough to shake hands.

I couldn't believe my nose. The scent was very faint — but unmistakable. It changed a lot of my plans for the meeting.

I shelved almost all the questions I wanted to ask. Instead I made the meeting about getting copies of security videos. I gave him a protected URL from Mason, and Phillips agreed to send copies of the last security videos of Alaska Brown and the earlier missing Alissa Barnett.

Then we sat at his master terminal, and I gave him the times and locations for when Judy was in the casino. We pulled up long shots so we could see the people around her.

Quickly I realized there was no point in seeking men who were watching her. Almost every male who saw Judy was watching her. It made me smile and gave me hope for when I become her age.

Assuming I live that long, of course.

Men who watched Judy were either outright smiling or had a crinkle in the corner of their eyes that indicated... what? Fondness? Yes, fondness.

So Phillips and I searched instead for stone-cold-sober looks in the people around her. We found one such man sitting nearby while Judy was chatting up a bartender. A cowboy at a nearby table watched her with soft, crinkly eyes, but the redneck at the end of the bar had a carefully blank look.

One other man caught our attention. He was a waiter in Georgio's Grille. He was serving tables while Judy was eating at the single's counter. There was one look right before Judy signed her check and left. Straight at her with no expression.

I had Phillips make me good printouts of the two men. And I got the name of the waiter-employee.

Then I leaned back in the chair. During this meeting, Phillip's eyes bothered me. Phillips would look at me then jerk his eyes away. Like he didn't want to look at me. I decided to ask Mason about it. It could be social ineptitude, geekiness. But probably not for someone at his job level.

"I have just one more question for you," I said. "Is George Moretti good at his job? Or is he just phoning it in?"

Phillips froze for a couple of seconds. His mouth opened, but he took another bit of time to speak. "I'm sure he's good, or he wouldn't be working here, would he? But I don't really know his job. I'm concentrating on doing mine."

I thanked him again and stood up. I leaned in and shook hands again, just in case I was wrong about the smell.

But I wasn't.

I waited until I was back in the office — on our secure server — to call Connor, who was in Wichita with Judy.

"How's Judy?" I asked.

"Having fun setting up this apartment."

He paused, then said, "She seems so fragile, but she could run circles around my old Army drill sergeant."

I smiled. Not many people could go from being attacked in their bedroom to single-handedly setting up a safe house the next day.

"I met with Jerry Phillips," I told Connor. "It was 11 AM, and he'd already had a hit of cocaine."

"What? How do you know?"

I thought about how to frame this. "Did you know perfume companies seek out people with the most sensitive noses in the world? And they pay them a bundle because so few people have the skill?"

"I didn't. I reckon this matters somehow?"

"Well, I have a great nose. In another life, I could be creating perfumes. Instead, I'm sniffing cocaine on Jerry Phillips. You can't mistake the smell once you know it — it's a mixed flower kind of scent combined with whatever they used to cut it. In Phillip's case, it was kerosene."

"Kerosene?"

"That's pretty common," I told him. "Other options include ammonia, baking soda, or sulfuric acid."

"Yuck. It was offered to me several times. The powder was right in front of my nose and I didn't smell anything. I thought it was scentless."

"It's only scentless to nose-blind people like you and 99% of the population. But the key point here is — Jerry used cocaine this morning. Before going to work. Which means it's a serious habit for him."

The phone was silent, then I heard Connor take a deep breath. "He can be blackmailed."

A door chimed over the phone. "Just a sec," Connor said.

Two minutes later, he was back. "Deliveries have been coming in all day."

"Connor, I'm going to leave investigating Jerry Phillips to you. With your contract with the casino, you can watch him much better than I can. You'll want to work with Mason — he can find out everything Jerry's been up to electronically. Plus his bank records."

"Mason's flying in here late to add more security. We'll both dig into Jerry tonight."

"I hope you won't be sleeping on the floor?"

Connor laughed. "There's two beds plus a pull-out sofa bed already here. You have to come see this place."

"After we find Alaska. Gotta go."

I hesitated, but it was something else Connor should know. "Just one more thing — kind of an FYI. You have a secret lie detector you can use if you need it. Me. My nose can also smell fear sweat."

"Fear sweat?

"If you ask someone a question and they lie, they give off a tiny little jolt of fear sweat. I'm about 99% accurate. I wanted you to know in case you need it with Jerry Phillips."

"That's a real advantage. You're full of surprises, aren't you, Flores?"

"You have no idea."

21

Sara Flores
Four Leaf Clover casino

The cashiers cage at the casino was a whole other level of weird. It made up one wall of floor-to-ceiling, bullet-proof glass for the huge card-game-tables room. There was no place inside the cage where the three women and one man working there would not be on full view. It was worse than what animals face in zoos — they, at least, usually had a den.

I wondered what it would be like to have 200 people watching every time you scratched your butt. Not that the people outside stared in often. The level of security guards around the area, uniformed and not, would make looking too long be very uncomfortable. Walking up toward the cage, I could see six or seven men turn unfriendly eyes at me from all corners of the game room. Like they were considering how fast and how damaging a response they might have to make against me.

My skin itched like I was surrounded by threats. The hairs on the back of my neck were standing at attention.

I'd arranged to meet with Rita Gutierrez — a woman I was

assured was Alaska's best work friend — at the end of her shift. I wanted to get her away from here because I didn't want to talk to her with 600 cameras watching us. I also suspected the casino had more than one lip reader on the surveillance payroll.

At 10 PM, promptly, a very slender woman about my 5' 7" height, came out of the door next to the cashier's cage. I recognized Rita Gutierrez from the picture Mason had sent me.

We shook hands, and I followed her to her car, then followed her car to the GOAT Bar and Restaurant. The GOAT had brown lacquered floors and bright turquoise seating. There was a mile-long stretch of bar seats curved around the bar with a few booths to the sides.

Happily, an end booth was vacant, so we grabbed it. I'd promised her food, drink, or whatever she wanted — which turned out to be coffee and a slice of mango key-lime cheesecake. I figured what the heck and joined her with a Diet Coke and some Lebanese baklava.

"Why did you ask me to leave my cell phone in the car?" she asked after we gave the waiter our orders. "You think the Four Star Casino has bugged my phone? That would be illegal, wouldn't it?"

"It would be illegal," I agreed. "Unless they put it in the fine print of your employment agreement. You had to sign something agreeing to all the cameras and listening devices at work. Maybe you also agreed to more — with some kind of language about if it were necessary to prevent or uncover a crime."

Her eyes opened wide.

I smiled. "Let's just assume I'm paranoid because of my P.I. work, and you're humoring me. Okay?"

"Is that why you were feeling around under the table?"

My eyebrows raised. "You caught that?"

"After seven years in a cashier's cage, I watch people's hands at all times. Yours disappeared under the table. I was pretty sure you weren't feeling for chewed bubblegum, so you were either searching for a bug or placing one."

The waiter came over with my soda and her coffee. Rita took a sip of hers as she watched the waiter leave.

"Are you having any luck finding Alaska? I miss her so much."

"Do you think she left willingly?"

"Not a chance. She'd never leave her kids. And she liked her life."

I sighed. "We've got a ton of suspects, but nobody stands out yet. One question we haven't been able to answer is whether Alaska had a man she was seeing. I was hoping you'd know."

Rita shook her head. "The police asked me that at the time, because of what Brittany told them. That Alaska hugged the man in the other van and got in willingly. But I'm pretty sure she wasn't seeing anyone. I told that to the detective. From everything she told me and I saw, she went straight home each night to her kids."

"We've been tracking her hours, and you're right. She went straight home after work. But she has extra, unexplained time in the mornings. Two or three times a week, she'd leave about an hour earlier than she needed to."

Rita shook her head and bit her lip. Tears sprang to her eyes.

"She wasn't meeting a man. She was meeting me. At Veterans Park. She wanted to get back in shape, so we were training for the Jenks Half Marathon race. But she never made it — she disappeared in September, and the race is in November. I thought about running it myself, but I just couldn't. I thought, 'I'll wait until she's home and we'll run it together.'"

Our desserts arrived. Rita scooped up a bite of her cheesecake and put it in her mouth. She closed her eyes and moaned.

I laughed. "If you want a little alone time with it, I can hit the restroom."

"It's my favorite dessert in the entire city," she said. "But you can stay. As long as you don't even think about asking for a taste of it."

"I wouldn't dare."

I left her to it for a few minutes until her eyes opened again. Then I got back to work. "Was Alaska having problems with anyone? At work? Elsewhere?"

"Nothing unusual. Our boss can be a jackass sometimes. He thinks you have to be bossy to be a boss. But Alaska and I've worked for worse. We mostly ignored him and it was fine."

I finished my dessert and started on the Diet Coke as a chaser to all that sugar and fat. "Anything happen in the last couple of weeks before she went missing. Anything no matter how small?"

Rita put down her fork and shook her head. "I've tried and tried to think of something, but I just didn't notice anything different."

"If your life depends on finding something small. Something that surprised you or ticked you off. Anything that seemed even a tiny bit wrong?"

She shook her head again. "Everything with Alaska was normal as far as I can remember."

"Everything with Alaska was normal? What about someone else? Did anyone else act different?"

"Not really."

I raised my eyebrows.

"I don't really know. It's just Brittany... the woman who saw Alaska get in the van?"

"Yes?"

"I saw her a couple of times in the restroom here. She always looked at me. Like... Well, I just assumed she was gay. Then she quits and runs off to Mexico with some boyfriend. So... I guess I was wrong. Or she swings both ways. It was a little surprising."

"Interesting."

"But she told everyone she was going with her boyfriend, right? And I heard they interviewed her in Mexico, and she said the same thing. So I must have just read her wrong."

"How sure were you — before you learned all of this about the boyfriend?"

"Pretty sure. Maybe 90-95% sure."

The waiter came with the check, and I left cash. "Thank you," I told Rita. "You've given us another angle." I gave her my card. "In case you think of anything else."

I walked her out to her car. "Please, Rita, don't go asking questions at work. Someone did that for us, and she was attacked. If you have questions, call me and I can get them answered."

Rita opened her arms and hugged me. It was a shock and took me a second to hug her back. "Thank you," she said. "Nobody was doing a damn thing about finding her after all this time."

"I won't stop." It was all I could truthfully promise her.

I drove home to my small, nondescript house that looks lower-middle class except for being surrounded on three sides by a U-curve in the Arkansas River. And except for my hidden security and surveillance system, that probably cost more than the house.

There was a full moon out, and I spent a minute looking at it — feeling the pull. I almost never transform unless I have to. The pain of it all is just too great.

Although... three times in the past two years, I drove my wolf-dog Skidi and myself out into the middle of nowhere and let the moon take me. We'd run and played the entire night as wolves, and I revealed in it — the sheer joy.

I smiled, remembering.

I was thankful that all the stupid werewolf books and movies were wrong — I didn't *have to* transform every full moon. I wanted to. The moon called to me. But I could always say 'no.'

I opened my door and gave myself a poor substitute by spending half an hour rolling around on the floor with Skidi, getting my face expertly tongue washed. Canines don't really like getting hugged, but I needed some hugs right then. Skidi tolerates my hugging her as long as it's part of wrestling and playing.

Then I got on the secure phone with Mason.

"I've got a new priority for you," I told him. "I know you didn't find anything suspicious in your first pass on this Brittany Rebane, who left for Mexico when Alaska disappeared. But dig deeper. Alaska's friend Rita thinks Brittany might be gay."

"So why quit her job to run off with a man...."

"Exactly. You got into the Tulsa PD computers once. I really need you to do it again."

"What do you want?"

"I want to know every interaction they had with Brittany. Any emails, any phone recordings, any meetings in Mexico or here. We need to find her and talk to her."

"Didn't the Lupiti cop say she got fed up talking to them in

Guadalajara? She dumped her phone there and must have gotten a new one."

"Yes. So see what you can find out about buying a new phone in Guadalajara — and if there's any way to find out how many were bought between the day before her phone shut off and three days after."

22

Sara Flores
Veronica Rebane's house in Tulsa

There are low-income houses that shine because of the care taken by the homeowner. A touch of fresh paint. A couple of flower boxes. A yard that is watered and mowed. Then there are houses that start out okay and go straight downhill from there. A yard loaded with junk on dying grass. Peeling and/or faded paint. Siding falling off.

Like the house right in front of me.

I double-checked my phone, but this was it. The house was owned by Veronica Rebane, a former Miss Tulsa and mother of Brittany. An old-style tan car with big wrap-around tail lights was sitting in the driveway. Its body looked like it had played bumper car in real traffic and lost. Multiple times. I took a picture and sent it to Mason with a question mark.

I patted all my concealed weapons — gun at my back, smaller gun in my boot, and knife on my other leg — before getting out. My phone dinged with a text from Mason.

2002 Chevy Impala. Veronica's car. More upscale than average in 2002.

Thx

Veronica Rebane had once been a beautiful woman — I'd seen the picture of her being crowned. She had big, wide-set eyes, a generous mouth and shiny long hair. She still had the first two, although those gorgeous eyes now had big red veins in them. Her hair was still long but needed washing.

"What do you want?" She stood in the door, blocking my look inside.

I inhaled through my nose, trying to determine if she had a man inside. One did live here, his male-hormone-smell was unmistakable. But if he were here now, he was asleep in a back bedroom. I also smelled vodka. People think it has no smell, but even in human form I recognized the odor.

If she hadn't already had a drink this morning, she must have bathed in the stuff.

I showed her my private investigator badge — it works so much better than just telling people you're a P.I. — and told her I was investigating Alaska Brown's disappearance.

"Your daughter Brittany was the last person we've found who saw Alaska. May I come in and ask a couple of questions?"

She shook her head. "I already talked to the police."

"Yes, I've spoken with them. But a couple of new questions have come up. It will only take a few minutes of your time."

"Sorry, I'm busy." Veronica started to close the door.

I put my hand on it. "Mrs. Rebane, my employer has authorized me to pay a small fee to compensate you for your time. $200 for 15 minutes?"

She looked at me, head tilted to the side. "$500."

I shook my head sadly. "I'm sorry, but I can't go that high. The most I'm allowed to offer is $300."

"For 15 minutes?"

"Yes."

"Show me the money."

I reached into my pocket and pulled out six $50s. I spread them out like a hand of cards. Veronica opened the door fully, stepped back into the room, and grabbed the money from me.

The living room was dark, with drapes closed and just one light on — a floor light with an old-fashioned side-table around it like a skirt. It was placed next to a well-worn La-Z-boy.

The place had some upscale touches from back around the same time she got the car, but nothing new had been added since. Except for a flat screen TV almost five feet long. On the coffee table facing the TV was a shiny white Xbox game console.

Veronica looked at her watch. "Fifteen minutes," she reminded me.

"Had you ever met the man she went to Mexico with? What was his name... Bobby something."

"No," she said. "Brittany was very secretive about her friends."

"Did she tell you she was going before she left?"

"Of course." Her eye shift told me that was a lie. She didn't lie well. I didn't even need my nose to confirm it."

"What was his last name?"

"I don't remember." Now her body shifted as well as her eyes. But... interesting. The fear scent had disappeared. She was uncomfortable... but not lying.

"She was over 18," Veronica protested. "I'm not responsible for keeping track of where she goes and who she sees."

"Of course you aren't."

Veronica looked toward the kitchen like she was looking for help. Perhaps from the vodka. Instead she leaned over the coffee table and picked up a pack of cigarettes. She lit it without asking if it would bother me. Like maybe she hoped it would hurry me out the door. Instead, I got a glimpse of a single red stone hanging from her neck. It looked like a pigeon-blood-colored ruby — the most prized color. It looked like it was one carat, which would have set her back about $2,000.

How do I know? I've always loved gemstones — especially rubies and emeralds. I marvel how warm they feel in my hand. Like they were alive. And... if I ever have to go on the run, I could carry a fortune in a very small bag.

"Have you heard from her since she left? Other than the one call the police have in their reports?

"No." She stared at me. Defying me to make something of that.

"Please describe exactly what she said and what you heard in the one phone call you received."

"She said she and Bobby were in Guadalajara and having a great time. She said she hated Oklahoma and might never come back. She said she loved me even though we'd had our fights. And she hung up."

"How did she sound? Worried? Frightened?"

"Happy."

"Did you hear anything in the background? Other people talking? Bobby? Car noises? Anything?"

Veronica threw her hands up theatrically. "I can't remember. It was ages ago. I didn't notice anything at the time."

She stood up. "Anything else? Your time's up."

I stood. "No, that's all I needed to ask. My boss will be satisfied."

She walked me to the door.

"May I..." I pretended to hesitate. "I couldn't help but notice that gorgeous ruby you're wearing. It's really a beauty."

Her eyes opened wide, but then she smiled and pulled it out from under her shirt and showed it to me.

"Oh, my," I gushed. "You have such good taste."

She smiled in agreement and shut the door on me.

I pulled out my phone as I walked to my truck and speed dialed Mason. "You ready? You sure you don't want to place a bet?"

"I'm ready," he said. "And I never bet against you. Which... is very smart of me because she's on the phone already... oh, shit."

My eyebrows went up. "What's wrong?"

"She dialed a burner phone. I'm triangulating... It's located inside the Four Leaf Clover casino... give me a second...."

I heard a bang over the phone like Mason had slammed his hand on a desk.

"It's gone. Completely. I'd say someone just removed the SIM card, stomped on it, and flushed it down a toilet."

"So we know someone at the casino was expecting her call? Probably the same one who gave her some cash for a new TV and a neck bauble." I explained to Mason about the two new items in a house that hadn't seen new money since the turn of the century.

Frustrated, I asked, "That's it? We can't find out who she called?"

"Sorry, but I haven't been able to hack into the casino's surveillance feeds yet. They've got better security on them than the FBI uses."

"But..." he added. "We do have a man inside there — Connor. And all he needs to know is which employees were in a restroom at this exact time."

"He'll have to make up a story about what he's looking for. Because Jerry in Surveillance is our best guess right now for who she called."

Mason laughed. "I'll bet Connor's good at stories. I'll call him. What's your next step?"

I shook my head. "There might be answers in Guadalajara, but I don't want to waste time going there if I won't be able to find them. Did the cops have the specific location in Guadalajara that she called from?"

"Yes. Two locations. One in a shopping area. Another in a warehouse district."

I got in my truck. "This is frustrating!" I said to Mason. "In our previous cases, we always had a clearer lead by now."

"Agreed. We have leads here, but they seem to be pointing in different directions."

"Guess I'm going to Guadalajara."

"Isn't it fortunate we have Connor on board, who can continue to press things here while you're gone?"

"Stop pushing, Mason. Yes, it's good for this case. But we didn't need him before."

"We needed him on our last case."

"I'm hanging up. I've got to call Judy to set up my trip."

"Yes… you do need to call Judy."

"Stuff it!" I punched off.

The problem with cell phones? You can't slam them down to hang them up.

23

Connor Rockwood
Parking garage at the Four Leaf casino

Connor sat in his SUV where he wouldn't be seen by anyone coming out of the casino — but where he could clearly see Jerry Phillip's gray Lexus. Jerry usually left his Surveillance Director job about this time — 3 AM.

Sara gave him the lead on investigating Jerry, but he wasn't sure that was smart of her. He didn't know much about sneaky investigating stuff like some of what she was doing.

He was more a direct-action kind of guy.

He'd got all the intel Mason could find — and it was a lot. On the surface, Jerry was living within his means, even with the Lexus and the fancy condo. But if you add in hefty cocaine purchases, Jerry had another source of money. Serious money. Mason told him cocaine habits cost two to four thousand a week. That's $8,000 a month minimum that Jerry had to get from somewhere.

He ran his hands over the dash of his new Chevy Tahoe — the Midnight edition. He loved it. First, because he was used to it — it's what he used in Special Forces. The Tahoe or the Suburban — both were big, tough, and easy to find parts and repairs. But he'd splurged on the Midnight edition. The ads called it "sinister," with it's all-black look that included the black mesh grill and black painted tires.

It was also practical. He planned to tail Jerry Phillips, and the Tahoe should disappear into the background. Be less likely to be noticed.

The lights flashed on Jerry's Lexus. Five seconds later, Jerry opened the driver's door, dumped a laptop case on the passenger seat, and buckled himself in. Connor waited until Jerry closed the Lexus door before starting his Tahoe.

He hoped Jerry wasn't driving home, but Connor was confronting him — at home or not.

Jerry Phillips soon joined I-244 East, and Connor tucked in three cars behind him. Glancing in his own rearview mirror, Connor noticed the different styles of headlights on the cars behind him. He suddenly wondered about the headlights Jerry could see in his rearview mirror. His black-on-black Tahoe might disappear into the night, but the headlights? They were distinctive. And it wasn't as if they could blend in among hundreds of other Tahoes on the same road. Tahoes weren't in the top 20 most popular vehicles.

Hell — it was something else to consider. If he decided to start his own P.I. firm, he might need another car with unremarkable headlights.

More sneaky shit to worry about.

Up ahead, Jerry moved into the right lane and then exited the freeway. Connor followed him through a few stoplights until he pulled into the parking lot of the Last Chance Saloon. Connor shook his head. With a name like that, he was surprised at the modest neon sign, no wider than the door it was over. It looked more appropriate for a local, neighborhood bar where a newcomer might stick out.

He gave Jerry five minutes, then opened the door. A long bar ran the full length of the room, leaving room for one row of tables alongside it. It was so dark he could barely see, so nobody noticed him except a cheerleader-looking girl behind the bar. She nodded and went back to serving drinks.

He didn't spot Jerry at first, so he wondered if he was taking a leak — or had slipped out a back door. But as he wandered toward the back, there was Jerry, sitting alone and looking down at his whiskey. As were most of the others back here — it seemed to be a place for serious drinkers not looking to socialize.

There was an empty stool beside Jerry, at the very end of the bar, where a man could sit with his back to a wall and see the entire room. Connor sat down in it, amused that Jerry was so busy staring into his glass that he didn't even notice.

Unfortunately, the cheerleader bartender wasn't working this section. Instead, he got the other one — a 50-something, paunchy guy with what was left of his hair in a long ponytail. Connor ordered a Boilermaker.

As he spoke, Jerry raised his head and turned to look at him, his eyes widening in recognition.

Connor sat tall in his seat, facing Jerry. He knew how intimidating his 6' 4", 240-pound, arms-like-tree-trunks size could be — and he knew how to use it.

Jerry: "What are you... How did you... Did you tail me?"

"Yep."

"But... Why?"

"We need to talk. Away from the office."

"What about?" Jerry asked, his voice rising into a squeak.

"Security," said Connor, who then leaned in close. Quietly, he added, "Women have to stop disappearing from your casino, Jerry. You can't hide it anymore."

"Me?" He squeaked. "I didn't have anything to do with it. And you'd better...." Jerry started to get up.

Connor grabbed his arm, jerking Jerry back onto his stool.

Leaning closer again, Connor said, "I know about the cocaine."

When Connor first met Jerry, he thought his skin was the whitest he'd ever seen. But now, in a flash, it became so white it looked painted-on-white like a Geisha's.

"Wha... what cocaine?"

Connor decided to bluff. "I have the test results back from your steering wheel. The residue was faint — but 100% there."

"Somebody else must have driven...."

"Yeah, right," Connor interrupted. "Except there's only your fingerprints."

"Searching my car is illegal unless you have a warrant. You don't have a warrant, do you?"

Connor shook his head. "Jerry, Jerry. You signed away all your privacy rights when you took this job. You know that."

Jerry sat there, his eyes scurrying, trying desperately to think up some miracle that could save him.

Connor let him stew. He looked around to make sure nobody was looking at them, then he said, "Fortunately for you, I don't give a shit about the cocaine. Except as it's related to women going missing. Which is how I figure you're paying for the stuff. Because you're not making enough money to be buying it."

He leaned his mouth right up to Jerry's ear, "So what's your role in disappearing these women?"

Jerry shook his head from side to side. Violently. "No, no," he said. "I can't!" His voice got louder.

Connor kept a firm grip on Jerry with his right hand while his left reached into his pocket and pulled out $30. He left it on the table.

He stood up, pulling Jerry up with him. "Hey, buddy," he said, loud enough for those nearby to hear. "Don't worry, it'll work out. Let's get out of here, and we can talk more." He walked them back down the bar and out the front door, with Jerry shaking his head 'no' the entire way.

"Let's sit in my car," he said, pulling Jerry around to the passenger side of his Tahoe. At the door, Jerry suddenly dug in his feet. "I can't," he said, looking horrified. "They'll *kill* me."

Connor pushed the fob button to unlock the door. From the corner of his eye, he saw a parked Caddy turn on its lights and move toward them. The passenger-side window started to lower, exposing a gun barrel.

Connor jerked Jerry by the arm, trying to pull them both over the front of the car — so the engine block could protect them.

Jerry resisted.

Bullets spit out from the gun, one after another. Connor's brain noted it was an AR-15. Semi-automatic. A gun favored by gangs.

Jerry became a dead weight, and Connor had to let go.

A bullet dug into his left thigh as he flipped himself over the hood and pulled his Glock 19. Squatting made his thigh hurt like a son-of-a-bitch, but he had no choice. He crouched behind the engine block — making himself as small of a target as possible.

The bullets kept coming, even though Jerry had to be long-past dead. It seemed they wanted to kill him as well.

When the gun stopped, Connor popped up and aimed. The window was closing, and the Caddy accelerated out of the lot. Connor fired several shots at the window, but recognized bullet-proof glass. He used the rest of the magazine's 15 rounds on the tires — until they were no longer visible — but the car didn't stop.

He moved around the SUV to Jerry, but there would be no last words giving up his dealer or the man who had bought him. Jerry looked like a very bloody piece of Swiss cheese.

Painfully, he sat down on his butt, taking the weight off his thigh. He took off his shirt and tied it around his leg, trying to slow the blood he was losing.

With a big sigh, Connor called Mason first, then 911 then, at Mason's suggestion, Detective Rodriguez.

While he waited, he pondered where this left the investigation. How could they find who was paying Phillips in coke? The shooters, those AK-15s, they all screamed gangbangers. Just like the two who came after Judy at her home.

But the brains behind this wasn't any gang boss. It was too big. They had people everywhere. Watching Judy in the casino. Tailing Jerry or him — or both — 24/7. Without being spotted. And they moved fast. Which meant enough foot soldiers available for immediate deployment.

He double-checked his phone to make sure it had recorded all of his conversation with Jerry Phillips. Then he emailed himself a copy of the recording.

He needed to talk to George Moretti, but he didn't have time before the cops — and hopefully an ambulance — arrived. Instead, he texted the man.

> Jerry Phillips dead. Coke involved. I found your security hole, so you owe me $40K. Will talk tomorrow after the docs and cops finish with me.

24

81 Days Earlier
Alaska Brown
Location Unknown

Three months had passed, but it felt like three years to Alaska Brown.

She knew it was three months because she'd made a tick on the wall each morning she woke here.

She sat on her disgusting mattress and rested her back against the wall. She needed to think, even though all she wanted to do was curl up in despair.

Miss Brenda had kept her alive to do all the scut work she would never do. Alaska had to prepare the food, clean, and take care of the three girls down here with her. Alaska was like a trustee at a prison — a prison that consisted of three plush cells, her bad one, a hallway, and stairs up. She had freedom of movement down here, whereas the girls were locked in their fancy rooms.

She knew why the girls' cells had beds and linens and actual toilets while hers didn't. She knew Miss Brenda wanted her to resent the girls. She probably wanted her to torment them herself. As if she would. At a minimum, Miss Brenda wanted her not to care what happened to the girls.

Alaska cared. But caring for the girls brought its own problems. This week, first Layla and then Grace had asked her to help them kill themselves.

She'd done her best for the girls over the past three months. She'd bandaged their cuts, set broken fingers, and applied cold, then warm compresses to terrible bruising. Tried to find favorite foods that would entice them to eat — and keep up their strength.

She'd held them in her arms when they cried and couldn't stop. When they told her to go away and curled themselves into little balls, she went back to her cell and swore the most vile curses she could imagine.

She'd never sworn before — she'd told her kids it was wrong. But if God thought there was anything wrong in her cursing now — well... she'd have a bone to pick with him. Such as why he allowed such evil people to live. Why he didn't smite them down.

Each girl was called upstairs at least once a week, only to return hours later in terrible physical pain — and even worse mental pain. The man's goal was apparently to debase them until there was nothing human left.

Worst of all was when he would come down to the dungeon. Always with tattoo man as a guard, or she would have attacked him months ago. He was 6' 2", but otherwise so ordinary. Thinning gray hair, glasses, face a little puffy, body slim except for the pregnant stomach many men get.

Once he wore a suit that probably cost more than her home back in Oklahoma. Although she could not let herself think about her home, or her kids, or her parents.

He usually wore slacks and a collared shirt — opened a button or two so he looked like an ordinary guy. Crocodile or snake-skin cowboy boots to prove he wasn't.

Which wasn't necessary. Even without the suit, the man walked like he owned the world. Like he used the bodies of the "little people" as rugs to cushion his walking. His accent sounded Texan, which fit her Oklahoma prejudice of arrogant-ass Texans. But he might not be a Texan — she tried to keep an open mind. Somewhere Southwest, but maybe not Texas.

His name? The girls said he made them call him God. Alaska thought of him as Satan.

Him coming down unannounced was why she had to keep the place spotless and odorless. She'd refused. Just once. As punishment, Miss Brenda gave her to the tat-man for a night. The next day, with a broken arm, one eye swollen completely shut, and internal bleeding, she cleaned the place spotless. You could eat off this damn floor from that day forward.

God forbid Satan had to endure a molecule of smell he didn't want. Although he seemed to like the smell of blood well enough — as long as he caused it.

When he came down, the girls had to stand at their doors. He'd walk between them and touch them — insultingly — like he was picking a side of beef for dinner. He'd torment them with his indecision before having his guard grab one of them and take her up with him. Only to send her down hours later, sobbing or almost comatose.

Alaska had been trying to stay alive. And to keep alive the hope of seeing her children again. Waiting for some change she could use to get out of here.

She'd given the three girls her full name — and got theirs in return. In case one of them got out and could tell the authorities. And the families.

As for helping someone suicide, Alaska just couldn't. Modern Catholicism said grave suffering or torture diminished the sin of suicide, but it was still a sin. And there was no clear reading on the sin of helping someone in anguish commit suicide.

She had to hope they'd get out of here one day. If she helped a girl commit suicide, and then they got out of here, she'd never forgive herself.

25

Sara Flores
Alebrije Hotel, Guadalajara, Mexico

The phone woke me up from a dead sleep, and for a minute, I couldn't remember where I was. There was a blue sky painted on the ceiling, fancy iron lights on the wall and red Saltillo tiles on the floor.

Right. I was in Guadalajara. Chasing two very tiny leads.

Judy had paid a fortune extra so I could park the Chevy Cavalier airport rental in this hotel's limited-space garage. I felt funny wasting the money. Usually, I just take cabs in a foreign city.

The Police were singing their creepy song, "Every Breath You Take," from my iPhone — which meant Mason was calling me. I took a second to rub my eyes and looked at the time. It was six AM.

This had better be important.

"Don't worry, everything's fine," Mason said.

Oh, hell. "What happened?"

He told me.

"Connor was shot?"

"He's going to be fine. It was a through-and-through, and it didn't hurt anything vital. He'll be home tomorrow, although he's supposed to take it easy on the leg for a few days."

I shook my head. "I thought I was being careful by planning to break with Connor and Judy after this one case. But they might not survive this case. They're not like you, Mason. You're not in the line of fire. And you're pretty well hidden. And even so I've worried about you."

Mason was quiet.

"So, who did this? That Adonis gang guy? Same as went after Judy?"

"Probably. But Adonis is not calling the shots. They're small-time thieves. Gangbangers. They aren't behind a multi-year disappearing women operation."

"Wait a minute. Just a minute. Let me understand. Connor made no contact all day with Jerry, correct?"

"Correct."

"Then he follows Jerry to a bar, joins him, they talk for a short time, then they go out to the car, and shooters are there to kill them? In less than an hour from when Connor first started the tail?"

Mason: "That's what he said. They must have been following Jerry or him — or both of them — for at least a couple of days. Maybe since they went after Judy. Or maybe back when he made the deal with George Moretti to investigate the casino's security."

"This case is really big," I said. "Bigger than I ever imagined. Whoever is behind this has a shit-ton of money and enough foot soldiers to be running his own private army."

"It's not really about Alaska Brown, is it?"

"No," I agreed. "This is a well-oiled machine making someone a fortune."

"Are you staying in Mexico or heading back to Tulsa?"

"Some part of their machinery was here, and maybe it still is. I'll look around today, but I'll probably be home tomorrow. Or, at the latest, the day after. Meanwhile, get me everything you can about everyone in the state of Oklahoma who's gone missing in the past five years — no, make it seven years — and hasn't been found."

"Anything else?"

"Tell Connor to hire one of his friends as a bodyguard. We'll pay for it. And don't let him give you any macho shit. If they still want to get him, they'll come in numbers. He needs backup.

"And tell Judy to find the best bodyguard firm in Wichita and hire one for the condo there. Wait… she's not there under her own name, is she?"

"No, we got her papers under another name."

"Thank god. I thought that was the case, but…"

"Calm down, Sara. It'll be good."

I held my head in my hands. "I can't be responsible for all these people. I don't know how to do it. I'm worrying about them when I should be focusing on here."

"Let's talk about there. I sent you the two GPS locations where Brittany Rebane's phone was. One was from when she called in. The other was from when the police called her. Right before the phone went dead."

I looked at my cell. "Check the nearby buildings for each location. See if any of them have an unusual amount of phone or computer activity compared to the neighbors. Text it to me when you find it."

"Right," he said, then his voice trailed off. "And… I'll also look for any nearby place with unusually high electric usage." He hung up on me.

I'd brought three knives with me to Mexico. I strapped on my normal Spyderco in a sheathe at the small of my back, and I added a Balisong in my right boot and 4" Stinger II dagger with sheath that straps on my left inner forearm and has a quick release button.

Was I feeling especially bloodthirsty? No, I just didn't want to bring a gun into the country. You can get them across the border pretty easily, but getting out of a Mexican prison if you're caught with one is much, much harder.

Also, I'd feel guilty bringing one in. Mexico hates the flood of guns coming into their country from the USA. We're smuggling in almost 90% of their illegal guns.

I shouldn't need a gun, anyway. At least, I hoped not.

26

Sara Flores
Streets of Guadalajara, Mexico

The morning here had been surprisingly cold for Mexico in April. But now, at 11 AM, it was pushing 90 degrees. I wondered how bad it would be in the summer but decided I didn't want to know.

The street corner where Brittany Rebane first called the police was in the historic area, just north of the Avenida Revolución. A tourist map of downtown districts called it the "as hipster as it can be" zone but advised against being there at night.

It was beautiful during the day. There were multi-colored umbrellas suspended across upper-story balconies — covering 30% of the hot-sun sky for those walking on the street. The umbrella pinks and yellows and blues not only cut the heat but filtered the light into something festive.

I stood on the corner and looked in all directions. No cars were allowed on this street, so at ground level there were only shops with intricately-carved doors, small cafés with limited menus, and lots and lots of tourists. Nobody who looked like a local sat in any of the three cafés on the adjoining blocks. This wasn't an area where a girl trying to stretch out limited funds — like Brittany — would hang out.

A text arrived from Mason.

> No nearby buildings stand out for unusual electric or internet usage.

I walked back to my Chevy and drove to the other location — where the cops had reached Brittany's phone for a follow-up conversation. The last time they would talk to her.

The scene here was industrial instead of touristy. But not big, shiny, new industrial like some areas I passed through. The phone had been halfway down a narrow street "paved" with dirt and stones. A line of work-horse pickup trucks and old SUVs lined both sides of the street. The solid wall of one building smashed against the next and the next on the block. None of them had windows, but each had a door — 15-20 doors on each side of the block — where multiple small businesses stored goods and whatever else they needed.

I walked both sides of the street and saw not a single name plaque for any of the doors. Just door numbers, sturdy doors, and locks. I took a few pictures and texted them to Mason.

Then I opened the NetSpot app Mason made me install on my iPhone. There were two visible private networks within reach of my phone — plus one hidden network. And, unlike some, the hidden network was encrypted.

Mason texted me:

> Encouraging
>
> > Maybe, but I don't see the right kind of place here.

I hadn't seen any traffic in 15 minutes, but it would still be a stupid risk to bring a girl in one of these doors. Whoever we were up against was not stupid.

> I'm going to walk behind these buildings.

I turned down a cross street and noticed there was no alley between it and the next street. The buildings on each street took all the available land and backed right up against each other. They had the maximum amount of interior space possible for the size of the land. The only way to add more square footage would be to add a second floor, which only a couple of the buildings had done.

The second street looked just like the one I'd left. Door after door — all with no windows. All with parked vehicles on the street.

I retraced my steps and continued past the first street to see what was behind the buildings on that other side.

Here I found a difference. Four of the buildings on this street had garage doors where a car could drive into the building. This made more sense for a kidnapping operation.

If there was something here. If I wasn't just wasting time.

I walked the length of that street, then back to the first, trying to look casual. It was a wasted effort. The temperature was now pushing 95 and the slight breeze was kicking dust into the air, making me spit dirt. The buildings looked abandoned. Nobody would be here for sightseeing.

I got back in my car and turned on the A/C at max.

MASON SPENCER
What do u think?

> If each door is a separate biz, there's about 50 in these 3 blocks. Only 3 of them have internet access—so it's rare in this neighborhood. & 1 of the 3 is a hidden network??

Agreed. Odds are the hidden network is for something illegal.

> Agreed. But... these spaces are tiny. & the signal is coming from a no-garage building — which wouldn't work. &... I saw no obvious security cameras anywhere.

So, your plan is to sit outside 24/7 & wait for someone to do something?

I laughed. He knew I couldn't do that.

> Maybe…

A glimmer of an idea came to me.

> Maybe… someone bought adjoining buildings here & broke thru walls. Turned 3 or 4 into one space.

> A warehouse with a garage could open inside to a warehouse without one — which could face the next street.

I buckled up and put the car into drive.

> I'm coming back here tonight.

27

Sara Flores
Guadalajara, Mexico

My watch said it was 1 AM local time when I drove back to the street where Brittany's phone had been — the street without the garages.

Nobody was around.

I lowered my car window and pointed my iPhone at each of the doorways on the street. I'd seen no obvious security cameras, but some could be here. Better hidden.

Security cameras at night emit infrared light. A video camera or phone with an electronic viewfinder — not an optical one — will capture infrared light. At least, that's what Mason told me, so it has to be true.

If cameras are here — even though I can't spot any — the light would show on my phone.

With no traffic, I was able to drive on the wrong side of the street, pointing my phone out the driver's side window.

No lights flashed on my phone as I drove down one side of the street so I did a U-turn and came back on the other side — the side backed up against buildings with garages. This time, halfway down the street, my phone lit up. Three beams of light from security cameras covered one ordinary-looking, beat-up door. One camera beam faced each side of the street, and one was directed toward whoever might be at the door.

Bingo.

I drove to the next block with the four garages and again drove by with my phone in video camera mode. One of the four garages had the same security camera setup — over the garage and the door beside it.

I drove to the end of the block, outside all the security beams. "I'm going in," I told Mason.

"And if it's some poor honest businessman?"

"I brought $2,000 in cash as an apology."

"And if it's not who we want but some huge drug cartel operation? You don't have any guns."

"Then I'm screwed."

"Sara!"

"Just kidding. Then I run. Maybe transform so I can avoid notice by being a dog. Mason... we need to know now. If we're wrong, I can't waste any more time here. If we're right — it's well past time to bring Alaska home."

I turned off the car.

I put in an ear bud and put in my earrings that doubled as microphones. I put the battery transmitter — thankfully small — in my jeans pocket.

"Soundcheck?"

"I hear you," Mason said. "Don't do anything I wouldn't."

"You always know how to make me laugh."

I placed the car key under a rock near the car, and a packet of beef jerky under the car. I dropped another packet behind the wheel of a well-used pickup truck on a side street.

Once I turn wolf, I need to eat meat to revert to human. Usually, that's not a problem, as I can take a chunk out of whatever bad guy I just killed. But if I transform in order to hide, the beef jerky is my insurance policy for when I want to turn back.

Then I walked straight up to the door with the cameras and knocked.

Nobody answered.

I knocked harder.

Again, nothing.

I pulled out my phone and found the security camera right above the door, its beam pointing straight at me. I looked directly into it.

"*Estoy buscando* Alaska Brown," I said to the camera, using my pitiable Spanish. Too bad my father disappeared when I was eight years old — or I could be fluent in the language.

Continuing on, but in English, I lied, "She was last seen inside this building, so I'm not leaving until I talk with her."

Okay, that was a double lie. Alaska was never seen here. Brittany wasn't either, but she called the police from here. Although she could have been outside on the street.

Still nothing.

I put away the phone and pounded my fists on the door like a child throwing a tantrum. As hard as I could. With my strength, I should have been damaging the door and the hinges — but I wasn't. Which meant the door was steel reinforced and the hinges were made of stainless or carbon steel.

So... no innocents behind this door. Would it be a drug cartel or the people behind these missing women? Or, god forbid, both? I was about to find out because I could hear someone pulling bolts back. I took out my private investigator license and held it in front of me.

The man who opened the door was just a little taller than my 5' 7", but he probably weighed enough for two of me. He was wearing a tight green-silk shirt that looked like he'd slept in it, jeans, and alligator-skin cowboy boots. His hair had been shaved from his starting-to-bald head probably four days ago, leaving stubble all over his head and jaw. It contrasted with his full mustache.

He looked up and down both sides of the street as though searching for others who came with me.

"¿*Habla English?*" I asked.

"No."

Oh boy. "*Soy una investigadora privada.*" I held up my private investigator license for him to see. "*Estoy buscando* Alaska Brown." I held up a picture of her.

He showed no recognition.

"*También, estoy buscando* Brittany Rebane." I showed her photo.

"*No la conozco,*" he said as he tried to close the door in my face.

Like hell he didn't know Brittany. I grinned because my nose told me he was lying.

"Oh, I think you do." I slammed the door in on him, pushing him back, forcing my way inside.

"I need to make sure neither woman is here," I said, "and then I'll be on my way."

There were a lot of big boxes in the front room — stacked haphazardly and loaded with dust. I pushed up on one of the top boxes, and it was so light it had to be empty.

Dummy boxes — to fool any visitors.

I quickly opened a door at the end of the front room so I could see what this space was actually used for.

It was curious that the man didn't try to stop me.

I soon learned why. As I entered an open 15x15 space, I heard him lock the front door behind us.

There was a desk in this space with three locked cabinets behind it. Three big, comfortable, leather-looking chairs were spaced on opposite sides of a colorful Mexican rug. The walls were clean white. The room was a shocking contrast to the first room.

A door to the right opened into what had to be the next-over warehouse space. I commented for Mason to hear, "Nice expansion here to the right. How many of the adjoining spaces did your business take over?"

No answer. I had no proof he understood English, but I was going to assume he did. He wasn't acting like some low-level goon. Instead he was watching to see what I did and what I knew.

I heard another set of footsteps behind me and smelled a second man. I did not smell gun oil — believe me, I tried — so either they didn't have guns or they weren't keeping them in good condition.

The next space over had been made into three rooms plus the hallway to access them. I saw three doors with locks on the outside. Each room had a barred window in the door. It looked like a row of prison cells, but oversized ones.

I looked through the first window and saw a full-sized bedroom. There was a twin bed with sheets and a blanket, a comfortable chair, and an open door that led into a small bathroom. A blonde woman was lying on the bed, slowly moving her head from side to side like she was Stevie Wonder listening to great music.

She was gorgeous. A mass of blonde curls, huge emerald-green eyes, and skin like a porcelain doll. She was wearing a t-shirt and gym shorts. No shoes.

I tried the doorknob, but it was locked. I held the knob tight and tried to rattle the door. Not using my strength — just testing it. It wasn't strongly built — there was no steel reinforcement here. But there was more to the door than some normal apartment hollow-core door.

There was an intercom thing right under the window. I pushed the button.

"Do you speak English?" I asked.

The woman's head stopped moving, and she turned her eyes to the door. She nodded yes, then her eyes glazed over and she resumed moving her head from side to side.

I pulled out Alaska's and Brittany's pictures and pasted them to the window. I glanced back to the doorway and saw the man just standing there. Watching. Willing to let me continue.

The second man wasn't visible, but he was near. Given how strong his acrid odor was, the man was probably just outside the hall door.

I pushed the intercom button again and asked, "Have you seen either of these women before?"

Her eyes came back to the window. I think she focused enough to see the pictures. But she gave no indication as to whether or not she recognized either woman.

Her head resumed its side-to-side movement.

Whatever drug she was on, it was strong.

I looked back again at the man.

He smirked and waved his hand at the other doors like a gentleman would say, 'After you, my sweet.'

Okaaay.

The second room was exactly the same as the first, except nobody was in it. I even knew nobody was in the private bathroom because I could see all of it from the vanity mirror. The view was distorted, however, because the "mirror" was made of polished stainless steel — not glass.

I nodded to myself. Glass could be broken and turned into a weapon. For use on someone else — or yourself.

The third room was on the end. This room was both bigger and better furnished. There was a small open closet door with clothes hanging inside. And there was light coming from a TV. I heard music — a woman singing about her heart or her lover, "*Mi corazon.*"

I tried the doorknob, but it was also locked.

I pushed the intercom button. "Hello?"

A woman poked her head out from the bathroom door. She was Hispanic and in her 20s. Pretty, but not stunning. Cheekbones that would cut like a knife. Not Alaska — even if Alaska had lost weight. Certainly not Brittany.

"Do you speak English?"

She cocked her head at me, as though I was some alien with antennae sticking out of my head.

She nodded yes.

"Have you seen either of these two women?" I put Alaska's and Brittany's pictures against the glass.

She shook her head no.

I wasn't getting any smells from the room so I couldn't tell if it was the truth. She didn't look or act like she recognized either woman.

I worried the two men would get restless and more men would show up. I wanted to see everything I could in this place before they tried to stop me. Because there's no way they were letting me leave — willingly.

Not after I saw women locked in rooms.

The most important question — were there other cages in these combined spaces? Where other women might be kept?

I turned and walked back toward the door leading into these cells. The man who'd been watching me moved to block the exit. Another man — the stinky one — moved into the doorway to also block me. This second guy was big and bloated — a giant.

28

Sara Flores
Warehouse in Guadalajara, Mexico

Confident I wasn't going anywhere with the giant blocking me, the first man moved several steps away from the door to the empty cell I'd seen. He opened the door and did his phony "After you, Sweetie" number by waving me to enter the room.

Delighted the two had separated, I smiled and moved toward him. I used the momentum to add force to my right fist, which I planted as deep into his solar plexus as I could — because I had to get past all that stomach fat and what were probably very hard abs beneath it.

His face winced with pain, then froze with fear as he couldn't breathe — either in or out.

It gave me enough seconds to throw him into the room and slam the door. I turned the key to lock him in, then quickly turned to the giant.

To my surprise, he was standing at the door, not coming to his partner's aid.

The giant smiled as if I were his pet mouse and had performed a cute trick for him. He even clapped his hands at me.

Apparently, he and the man I'd just locked up were *not* BFFs.

Standing there, trying to figure out what to do next, the Jack Reacher novels jumped into my mind. One thing that always impressed me was the warning he gave bad guys. He tells them that if they attack, they will end up in the hospital. *If* he's in a merciful mood.

This is not a tactic that will work for a 5' 7" woman. Actually... it's a tactic guaranteed to make a man like the one in front of me laugh his head off.

I needed a way to get past him that didn't risk us ending up on the floor with him on top of me. Even with my enhanced strength, I wasn't winning that one. Not unless I transformed and used my teeth — which wouldn't be smart before I checked out the rest of these spaces.

The man's smile grew bigger. He planted his feet in the doorway, held out his hands palms up, and gestured with his fingers. Telling me to 'bring it.'

Now that was just insulting.

I simply could not think of a single way I could get past him that wasn't lethal.

Then I gave myself a mental slap on the head.

Idiot, I told myself. Why was I worrying about not killing a man who had women locked in cells and for sale?

I smiled back at him and raised my hands in surrender. I walked toward him slowly, hands raised. As I got close to him, I lifted my hands higher toward his cheeks. I looked into his eyes like a lover, like a blind woman wanting only to touch.

There was longing in my eyes. A slight trembling in my hands.

His face moved toward my hands. For just a second.

Before his brow furrowed, his eyes hardened, and his fists came slamming into my ribs.

I was astonished to see my fingernails become wolf claws. They'd never turned before without my willing it. I could transform my hands into paws, sure. But this? I now had human hands with wolf-claw fingernails.

But I couldn't take the time to marvel at it.

The claws dug into his cheeks, securing his face, pulling it down toward me. Then my thumbs — also with claw nails — dug deep into his eyes. Deep down all the way to the bottom of the eye sockets, scraping bone. Down even farther to the small opening in the back of the eye socket.

He screamed and tried to back away, tumbling backward onto the floor and landing me on top of him. My right hand let go, but my left claw was trapped. Inside his eye.

Shooting pain in my left side made me cry out. His fist had damaged one or more ribs there.

"Damnit!" So much for doing this the easy way.

I forced my fingernails to return to human shape, and — finally! — I was able to pull my left hand from his eye.

The man had stopped screaming and thrashing. He was just lying there, moaning.

I reached into my pocket and fastened two zip ties together so I could fasten his wrists behind his back. Then I fastened three of them together so I could do his ankles.

Standing up made me gasp in pain. I touched my left ribs.

"Damnit. Damnit. Damnit."

The ribs would take a day or two to heal unless I could transform.

I hoped I wouldn't regret leaving the two women here while I searched the rest of the building, but the drugged woman needed more help than just an unlocked door.

The rest of the space consisted of storage, desk space, a computer room with serious audio equipment, and a scary room with hooks on the walls, a floor drain, and dark stains all over it. There was also a garage with three nondescript cars and room for three more.

Nobody else was in the place — something I expected to change at any time.

I went back to the office and sent Mason pictures of it. He had me call him from one of the phone setups, and he was quickly inside their computer system.

There was one locked file cabinet, which I broke into. I grabbed papers that looked important, although I doubted they'd have the most important information — who was running this operation. There were no photos of any women in the papers.

Mason found their security backup in the cloud and deleted all the video for today — deleting me from ever having been there. Then, once he had a copy of all their records, he sent a virus into their system and their cloud storage.

I ran back to the room with the two women. The blinded man was lying still, except for the movement of his breathing. I ran past him to the door of the larger bedroom.

The dark-haired woman was standing right by the door, trying to look out. She could see the giant lying on the floor.

I pushed the intercom and asked, "Do you want to get out of here?"

"Please!"

I unlocked the door. She came out cautiously, walking to the man on the floor, looking down at him. Then she swung her foot and kicked him hard — so hard she would have broken toes if she weren't wearing shoes.

"I need your help," I said.

"Sure. What do you need?"

I frowned. There was something... No time.

"There's another woman locked in. She's been drugged. Can you help me rescue her?"

"Yes. Yes. Quickly. We need to get out of here."

I nodded my head. But... I had this nagging feeling there was something I was missing. Something I really needed to know.

I unlocked the door to the blonde's room.

"Do you want to go?" I asked the blonde. She looked at me and the other woman, her eyes going wide.

She nodded. Slowly at first, then stronger and stronger. But she stayed on the bed.

I reached to lift her up and my ribs screamed at me. I turned to the dark-haired woman. "Can you help her get to my car? Then I can drive you somewhere, or you can go on your own. Whatever you want."

Quickly, we were out the front door. My Chevy rental was a block away.

The exercise or the night air was helping the blonde — she didn't seem as out of it. She moved on her own but stumbled often. The brunette held her up when she did.

I thought about asking the brunette's name but decided not to. I led the way, looking for trouble but seeing none.

Mason's voice came into my ear. "Gee, it's too bad you don't have a big tough partner there to help you. Isn't it?"

"Stuff it," I hissed at my button. So what if I'd just been thinking the same thing.

And... what the hell was I going to do with the blonde? I'm alone in Mexico. If I drop her off at an embassy, they'll get my car license plate. I am not getting tangled up in their legal system.

We reached my car, and I got the brunette to lay the blonde on the back seat. She closed the door.

I asked, "Are you coming with me, or do you want to go?"

"I'm going. Thanks."

I nodded. I let her start to turn away, feeling her freedom, before I said, "Wait. You're going to need money, aren't you? To get away?"

She turned back to me.

"I can give you $1,000 U.S., but it's back at my hotel. If you can help me get her..." I nodded at the woman lying on the back seat... "into my hotel room, I can give you the money."

She looked at me. Evaluating.

I said, "My ribs are cracked," so she'd see me as no threat. And I told her, "I'm worried you won't get far enough without money."

She nodded and got in the passenger seat. I started the car and drove to my hotel.

Mason's voice came softly into my ear. "Gee, aren't you glad Judy rented you the car — with garage access?"

I ignored him. My mind was scurrying. I had no idea how I was going to pull this off.

29

Sara Flores
Hotel, Guadalajara, Mexico

The brunette got the blonde into the garage elevator, holding her against the wall in case she passed out. Trying to make it look like she got drunk on a girl's night out.

Fortunately, nobody joined us in the elevator. And nobody was on the second floor when we exited.

"Just put her on the couch," I said after opening my room. I walked back to the closet. "I'll get your money."

Inside the closet, where the brunette couldn't see me, I reached into one of my hidden pockets and pulled out half of the U.S. dollars I'd stashed there before tonight's mission.

I came out and saw she'd moved to stand in front of the door. She was tapping a foot and looking like she wanted to run.

Holding out the money with my left hand, I walked to her.

"Thank you," I said. "I'm going to let her sleep it off, then see what she wants to do. But you helped."

She reached for and took the money. I brought my right hand up to my left shoulder, rubbing it.

As fast as my superior reflexes could move, I sliced the edge of that hand through the air and hit the left carotid artery in her neck. She dropped like a rock.

I smiled. I hadn't tried that move in two years — not since I used it on a Texas sheriff. It knocks people out for about a minute. That's enough time to transform into wolf, as I did in Texas.

Or it's enough time to get zip ties on a person's hands and feet and a gag in her mouth. As I did this time.

I started to pick her up, but my ribs reminded me that was a very bad idea. Instead I dragged her to an upholstered armchair and grabbed another zip tie — fastening her legs to one of the chair legs.

She moaned as I finished, and her eyes opened wide. She looked at her fastened hands and tried to struggle. Interestingly, she didn't try to scream.

I pulled another chair around to face her and sat down. "I'm still going to let you go and still give you the $1,000. But I have a few questions I need answered first."

I got up and walked behind her back to the closet. Quietly, I said, "Mason?"

"What's going on?" he asked.

"Are you still recording me?"

"No, I stopped when you got into the car."

"Turn it back on. I'm going to question the girl. See if you can match her voice to anyone."

"Sara?"

"Not now."

I went to the front door where the brunette had dropped the $1,000 when she lost consciousness. I picked it up and returned it to her. She had pockets in the front of her pants so I tucked the bills into one of them. She watched me with brows furrowed.

"I'm going to remove this gag. If you yell or scream, I'll shove it right back. I just want to ask you about that place you were held. About the men there. OK?"

She nodded.

I removed the gag and stood there, just in case she wasn't as smart as she looked. She kept her mouth shut.

I sat back down. "What's your name?"

"Carmen. Carmen Guadalupe."

I looked at her. "You're never getting out of here if you lie to me."

"I *am* Carmen Guadalupe. I choose that name."

"What's your birth name?"

She was furious with me. Her mouth puckered up like she was tasting something revolting. "Iliana Sanchez."

"Thank you. Now, Carmen, tell me everything you know about what was going on there. What were they doing? Who are they?"

She shrugged, lifting her zip-tied hands. "I know nothing. They grabbed me and locked me up in there. Ages ago."

"How many men have you seen there?"

"Three. There is Diego, the *pendejo* you beat." She shook her head. "How did you do that? He scares everybody. Even men."

"Who else besides Diego?"

"Hector. He was there tonight. What did you do with him? Did you kill him? Please tell me you killed him."

I shook my head. "Who else?"

"Ramon. He is only there some days. When Diego or Hector is gone."

"Diego, Hector and Ramon. Last names?"

She shook her head. "I never learned them."

"How many women have you seen? In the cells?"

"I don't know," she told me. "Lots. They cry when they first go into the cells. Or bang on the door. Later they stop. Then they go away, and new women come in and cry."

Mason's voice came suddenly in my ear. "Holy shit! Holy shit! She's Brittany Rebane? It's her voice — definite. But... it's not really her, is it? You knew?"

I smiled. "I guessed. Thanks for the confirmation."

Improved hearing was something else to thank my wolf for. Usually, it's good for hearing things too quiet for human ears. But in this case, when I heard Carmen speak, she sounded familiar. Like the voice recorded by the police when they supposedly interviewed Brittany. From Guadalajara. A voice I was allowed to listen to.

Suddenly, I realized something, and I swore in a low voice. "That bitch."

"Sara?"

"Brittany's mother. The cops had to play that tape for her and she had to know it wasn't her daughter. But she never told them."

Mason was silent.

"When we solve this," I told him, "you make sure the cops learn about what she did. Okay?"

"Count on it."

I returned my focus to Carmen. Her brows had furrowed. She knew I was talking to someone else. She looked around as if to find a microphone. She was not a woman to underestimate.

"Okay, Carmen," I said. "Let's go back to the one other lie you told me. That you've only seen three men there. In all this time."

She sat back in her chair. "Only three men I see. Others I hear."

I cocked an eyebrow at her.

"They bring in men to see the women. Sometimes one man. Sometimes more."

"To see them? Or fuck them?"

"Hah! They do not get their money's worth if they fuck. They stay only five minutes. Ten at most."

"How many men?"

She shrugged. "Every week, at least one. Often more."

"Different men?"

She nodded. "Different voices."

Mason came back in my ear. "There are six vehicles surrounding the warehouse you just left. I'm worried the cops could find your rental car was there — there's for sure a GPS in it. And if our bad guys own one or more of the cops... You might need a quick exit."

"Understood." But there was so much more I needed to ask Carmen.

I turned to her. "We don't have much time. There are six vehicles at the place where you were held."

Carmen's face turned white. I could literally see the blood leave her skin to run and hide.

"I know you made phone calls for them. You pretended to be the woman whose picture I showed you earlier."

"I had to," she said. "I had two jobs: call people pretending to be having fun in Mexico. And fuck Hector. If I don't, Hector gives me to Diego. Women Diego gets are never seen again. Diego talks to me sometimes. Tells me what he does with his women. I would pray for a way to kill myself."

"Decision time," I told her. "Stay here or come with me to the United States."

"What would happen there?"

"We can talk in the car. I need to steal some different plates for it."

"Better to steal a different car."

"Yes," I agreed. "But I don't know how."

"I can do that."

I looked at her.

"Some days stealing a car was the only way to eat."

"Okay." I cut her free from the zip ties. "Go down to the garage and find something you can steal. Not a rental car! I think they can be tracked."

"Can you…"

"Now! No — wait." I ran to my bag and pulled out a pair of super-thin gloves. "No fingerprints," I told her.

She nodded and pulled them on. As she turned for the door, I noticed her pat her pocket where the $1,000 was stuffed. She could take her chances on her own, but she had to know the U.S. would be safer for her. And what I had in mind wouldn't work unless she was willing.

I picked up my bag, threw in all the bottles of water I could find, then turned to the woman still lying there on the sofa, her head moving to music only she heard. Tentatively I pulled her to her feet. When she sagged, I put an arm around her waist and cautiously lifted to keep her upright.

It hurt — but the pain no longer took my breath away. It was tolerable.

I love being a werewolf!

As I moved us to the stairs, I wondered if Carmen would be in the garage. Or gone.

30

Judy Street
Wichita, Kansas

Judy Street was curled up on the new chocolate brown sofa she'd bought for the Wichita safe house. She had two physical books plus four she'd downloaded to her iPad and had bookmarks on her laptop for three websites. Her Persian cat Lola was purring beside her.

The place needed a fireplace, she thought. But she'd used up her budget to furnish it. She'd done pretty good, considering. And it's not as if she were moving here. As soon as they solved this case, she'd be back in her Tulsa apartment — which was decorated *exactly* as she wanted.

She pulled her mind back to the books and websites. They were all about taxes. Somebody on the team had to consider how to keep them out of jail.

As far as she could figure it, Sara and Mason took a bunch of cases for people who couldn't pay much or at all. Like the Stintsons and their daughter Alaska. Mason had told her about a few of the other cases they'd had, and the clients were like the Stintsons — poor.

So... where did all the money come from? She'd researched Sara and Mason online and neither of them came from money. They hadn't won any lotteries, either. There were really only two choices: they stole the money or they had anonymous benefactors who gave hefty donations so the team could help those who couldn't afford it.

Judy considered. Did she care if they'd stolen the money? She wasn't sure. She cared very much about the kind of cases they were taking.

But... either way, cash was coming in.

Now that they were establishing a P.I. firm, how were they going to account for the money? Judy thought at first they should become a nonprofit. But the government scrutinized those much more closely than small businesses. No, she decided. It needed to be set up as a small business.

Judy thought it was believable that many people would pay a private investigator in cash. So the business could declare some of this cash — wherever it came from — as income. They could keep the amount just slightly more than their expenses. Stay under IRS radar.

Her cell rang. It was Mason.

"How fast could you get a private plane to Guadalajara, Mexico? Preferably not at the main terminal. Sara's in trouble, and she might have one or two other women coming back with her. Without any papers."

"Budget?"

"Whatever it costs."

"Get off the phone, and I'll find out."

"No, Judy... on second thought, don't find out. Just make it happen." He hung up.

Oh my, she thought, grinning. *I love this job.*

31

Sara Flores
Streets of Guadalajara, Mexico

When the elevator doors opened, at the garage level, there was an older model blue Ford waiting for me — with the motor running.

Carmen jumped out of the car and took the blonde from me, loading her into the back seat.

"You drive," she said. "I am very bad driver."

She jumped into the passenger seat, and I got in behind the wheel. "Look for a parking lot," I told her. "Someplace by a store or restaurant or business where we can park the car and be one of many."

I pulled out from the hotel and hit a main street, turning in the opposite direction from where the warehouses were.

Carmen pointed out small eateries that were already open, but I wanted to put at least five miles between us and the hotel.

"There," Carmen said. "Up ahead. Big shopping mall. Parking underneath it."

I entered a ramp down. Even though the mall wasn't open, there was a clump of 20-25 cars on the first level by one elevator. I backed in between two cars and shut off the motor. The huge fluorescent fixtures above us lit up the area with blue-tinted light. I could see everything.

"Mason," I said. I heard static. "Mason?" I tapped my broach. And earrings. Hell, I couldn't lose him now.

How long had they been active? Maybe too long?

I reached in my bag and grabbed my wallet. Mason had sent me something that looked like a credit card, along with two tiny cables. I connected it to my broach using the tiny cable pins. A small red light went on. The card was recharging my broach.

Then I called Mason on my cell. "Update, please. How the hell do we get out of here?"

"I'm bringing Judy on," he said. "Go ahead."

Judy's voice came into my ear. "I've got a helicopter charter company ready to take you as soon as it's light out, which should be in 30 minutes. Don't wait too long to leave. Rush hour starts about 6:30 AM there, and you don't want to be in it. Your chopper is already parked on the roof of the BIVC Bank." She gave me the address.

"They'll fly you to San Luis Potosí. It'll take about an hour. The fastest I can get a private charter jet there is two hours. You might have a 15-30 minute wait in San Luis Potosí."

I asked, "The jet will take us directly to Tulsa?"

"Yes. As for your two passengers, I'll have our attorney meet you at the jet in Tulsa."

"Our attorney?"

"Atticus Snowden. Mason said you've used him before. With the price he quoted me, the man must be able to walk on water."

I smiled. "You're right. He'll be perfect." I was about to hang up when I heard her mumble, "Thank you, Judy, you're amazing."

I grinned. "You *are* amazing," I told her.

My phone's GPS gave me the route to the bank and estimated it would take 30 minutes. I waited five before turning on the car and pulling out of the garage.

Rush hour had not yet started, thank God, but there was enough traffic to blend in. The route took us around one of the huge traffic circles in the city.

Carmen interrupted my thoughts. "They will put me in jail?" she asked. "In the U.S.?"

"Not jail," I said, though I wasn't 100% sure. "They'll keep you for questioning, so they can learn everything you know. But you're coming here voluntarily — that's key. You're coming — at great risk to yourself — to help them stop a trafficking ring kidnapping American women."

A red light stopped me. "On second thought," I said to Carmen, "just do whatever the attorney tells you. He's much smarter than me."

The green light flashed, and I sped up. We'd gone about two blocks when a car swerved right in front of me.

I slammed on the brakes and felt for my gun — except I didn't have one. What idiot thought it would be a good idea to be here without one?

Oh, yeah. That was me.

I looked everywhere, but it wasn't part of an attack. Just some suicidal driver. I said thanks that nobody was close enough behind me to hit me and thus attract the cops. Drivers here were almost as crazy as New Jersey drivers — who were the worst in the world in my opinion.

As I got back up to speed, Carmen leaned over the front seat back. The girl in the back had rolled right off her seat and into the footwell.

"Is she okay?"

"Yes." Her arms strained as she lifted the girl back up on the seat. "There, there," she crooned. "Don't cry. You're going to be fine. Everything is fine."

"Does she look presentable?" I asked. "We're going to have to get her up an elevator and into the helicopter."

"I need some water."

I reached into my bag, which was tight against my side on the seat, and handed Carmen a bottle of water." I looked in the rearview mirror. Carmen took the hem of the girl's tank top and used it to wet and wipe dirt from her face, as well as a trickle of blood from her nose.

Carmen finished, then sat back down in the front. She turned to me. "What if *el Jefe* buys these police of yours?"

"*El Jefe?*"

She raised her hands. "I never met him. But I listen to everything Hector say about the big boss. Hector says he owns the police. And the politicos."

I turned where the GPS told me. The touristy areas with cafes and clubs disappeared, and the sky turned from black to charcoal. Enough to see the outlines of buildings. Now I could have been driving in Manhattan through tunnels made by skyscrapers.

'Sky scratchers,' my father used to call them in his translation from Spanish. It's one of the few things I remember about him — because it seemed so funny to the seven-year-old me. I pictured tall buildings reaching up and scratching the sky, like you'd scratch the chin of a cat.

Carmen tapped me on the shoulder. "Hey, you. What's your name?"

I winced and smiled. "Sorry. I'm Sara."

"The police?"

"We've hired you the best criminal attorney in Tulsa. You'll talk to him first. We'll pay for it as long as you tell him everything you know. The truth only." I stared at her.

She nodded.

"Then you'll talk to the FBI. An honest man I trust."

"Good."

I saw the bank building up ahead. I had to almost circle it to find the entrance to the underground parking lot.

I parked close to the elevators and left the keys and the parking ticket clearly visible on the dashboard. Hopefully... someone would steal it. But if not, at least Carmen and I were wearing gloves the entire time.

We got the blonde out of the car. She could stand — sorta — as long as she was leaning against something. But she was wearing just shorts and a tank tee. No shoes. If we had to stop on the ground floor and there was security... which there might be since this was a bank...

I'm terrible about sizes, but maybe... I grabbed my bag and pulled out my only other shoes, a pair of Nikes.

"Hold her," I said and knelt down and grabbed one of the

blonde's bare feet. It slipped into the shoe easily. Too easily. I tightened the laces as much as I could, then did the same with her other foot. For good measure, I grabbed a t-shirt of mine and pulled it over her tank. She was still inappropriate for a bank, but maybe no longer call-the-cops-immediately bad.

The elevators from parking went up only to the ground floor. While it rose, I turned to Carmen. "Give me the Spanish for 'helicopter' and 'reservation.'"

"I can..."

I interrupted her. "No, it's better if I talk."

"*Helicóptero* and *reserva*."

The elevator doors opened on a typical sterile corporate entrance — all chrome, steel, and tinted-glass floor-to-ceiling windows. There was no security. I found the directory, and we got into an elevator. Two men got on with us, but they weren't high on my threat index. They both gave the blonde a very careful once-over, with enough attention to detail that they should have been able to draw her from memory later.

We escaped them on the fifth floor, where we found the office for Helicópteros de Guadalajara. Carmen sat the blonde down on a real leather sofa and sat beside her so she wouldn't lie down and sleep.

I walked to the desk.

"*Buenos días*," I said, slowly and carefully, as a non-Spanish speaker trying to be polite and use the local language. I pulled out my U.S. passport and laid it on the counter.

"*Soy Sara Flores. Tengo reserva por helicóptero.*" I looked at my watch to hint I was running late. He looked down at some papers, made a checkmark, then looked back up at me.

"*Tres gentes?*" He looked dubiously at the two women who came in with me. I turned back to look. I could see his concern. Carmen had somehow gotten a line of car grease on her white capris pants. As for the blonde... In addition to clothes that looked like she'd slept in them, a trickle of blood was showing below her nose from her fall off the back seat.

"*Sí*," I said and stared aggressively at him. Would he dare to insult a customer?

"Is she alright?" he asked, assuming my bad Spanish made me a likely English speaker. He sounded actually concerned for the girl. In addition, of course, to concern about whether there was anything illegal going on here.

I rolled my eyes and tightened my mouth. "She's just fine except for being stupid and half drunk. We have to get her back to San Luis Potosí fast so we can sober her up. She could lose us our jobs!"

He nodded, but he was only half buying it.

I looked at my watch. "We need to go now. Is it ready?"

He looked at his paperwork. I hoped it showed the ridiculous amount of money I'm sure I was paying for this, because such an amount could ease qualms. Then he nodded. He handed me three tickets and escorted us back to the elevator. He pressed the "up" button to the roof.

We stepped out on the roof, and the helicopter engine started. The pilot looked at us as we got in and gave a startled look to the manager. I saw the small, tight nod he gave the pilot.

We buckled in — Carmen did the buckling on the blonde — and we lifted off. I watched the manager we left behind until he was too small to see. I knew damn well if we'd tried to take a bus, we'd be talking to the police.

I watched Guadalajara get smaller and smaller, and within 10 minutes, we were seeing land. Arid land, sectioned-off land, but also green land. Cliffs dropped down from flat, farmable land into a green canyon fed by a meandering river that we followed to the northeast.

The question was — did our money buy the helicopter manager's complete discretion, or would he call someone while we were in the air?

32

Connor Rockwood
Four Leaf Clover Casino, Tulsa OK

George Moretti had told Connor that Gene Alderman wanted an oral report instead of a written one. So the two of them rode the casino elevator up to the top floor where Alderman's office was.

"We're in the little conference room," Moretti said. He knocked on a door, then opened it and escorted Connor inside.

It might be the "little" conference room — the round table only had eight chairs — but it was still designed to impress. There was a wall of windows overlooking downtown Tulsa — literally overlooking. No nearby building was as high. Another wall held six video screens that were showing live action from the casino floor. The table was made of one of those exotic woods — polished to gleam.

An unknown man was in the room, back to them, staring out the windows. His back was straight enough for military service, but his suit cost more than Connor's Chevy Tahoe. Maybe more than two of them. The conservative cut and custom stitching screamed old money. Inherited money. Harvard or Yale, at least third generation.

Gene Alderman greeted Connor and shook his hand. Then he

walked them to the window and introduced Connor to Winston Bainbridge III, who headed up operations for all Bainbridge Casinos. The guy looked a lot like George W. Bush — short and with that casually polished look mastered by the rich. Unlike GWB, Bainbridge had an extra 60 pounds that puffed out his cheeks like a squirrel stashing walnuts. He had a full head of white, patriarchal hair, which contrasted with Alderman's bald pate.

Bainbridge nodded at Connor, shook his hand, and motioned for him and Moretti to join the two of them at the table.

"Just call me Winston," Bainbridge said. "Sounds like you did us a very big favor here. Tell us about it."

Connor described the events of the past few days and his last conversation with Jerry right before he was shot.

"How badly were you hurt?" asked Winston.

"I'll be good in a couple of days," Connor said. "Just a flesh wound."

Gene Alderman furrowed his brows. "So you think this is connected to the two women who went missing from here?"

"Yes. And it's probably three women, not two. Someone else was pretending to be Brittany Rebane when she talked to the police from Mexico."

Gene looked over at Winston. "I hadn't heard anything about this. Did you?"

Winston shook his head.

"You will in a couple of days," Connor told them, wondering if he should have kept his mouth shut about it.

Winston cocked his head at Connor. "You appear to have very good contacts."

Connor nodded. "I've done some work with the investigators that were hired to find Alaska Brown. Her going missing was one of the reasons I contacted your firm about doing a threat assessment."

"And we're grateful you did," said Winston. "One other question — how did you get onto Jerry Phillips?"

Connor decided to keep the onus on himself. He twisted his mouth in a rueful smile. "I happen to have a very sensitive nose. I smelled just a hint of cocaine on him while our heads were together — looking at surveillance feeds. It gave me a place to start."

"Well, good job," said Winston standing up. The others stood as well.

"Give the man his check, Gene. He's earned it."

Alderman handed him an envelope with the $40,000 check inside.

Winston pulled out a business card and handed it to Connor. "Give me a call. I'd like you to do your threat assessment on a couple of other casinos we have."

"Thank you, sir," said Connor. "I will."

33

Sara Flores
San Luis Potosí, Mexico

A half an hour into the helicopter flight, the blonde started coming out of it. Her eyes got big, and she looked around in surprise at being in the air. She turned to me and opened her mouth to question. I put my finger to my lips and shook my head. Although… the noise was so loud inside the copter that she probably could scream "fire," and nobody would know what she said.

I turned to the pilot and touched his over-the-ear headset, miming I wanted one for myself. So I could talk to him. He hesitated, then pulled out a set and handed it over. I gave it to Carmen and asked her to see if he had some paper we could write on. For work.

She rattled off some quick Spanish, and the man handed back paper and a pen, then motioned for her to return the headset. I shook my head. I wrote on paper for Carmen, "Keep until ride is over."

She fired off some rapid Spanish with a grin, and shoulder shrugging, making up some kind of story. She was good at stories.

I turned to the blonde and wrote "Sara Flores" and "Tulsa USA" on the paper and pointed to myself. Then I pointed at her and gave her the paper.

She wrote "Emma Wallace — Albuquerque."

I wrote, "Want to go to the USA now?"

She gave a definite nod, although it wasn't as frantic as I'd expected.

I wrote, "Pretend we're friends." I pointed at myself and my name on the paper. I wrote "Carmen" and pointed at Carmen.

Emma nodded.

I tapped Carmen on the shoulder as she was looking out and down at the scenery, which was half and half brown land interspersed with the deepest, darkest green — most of it in perfect squares, rectangles, and circles. The green looked like smooth, soft felt.

She looked at me. I tapped Emma's name on the paper and then pointed to her. Carmen nodded.

I pulled out my cell phone surreptitiously, because the pilot had told us to not use them during flight. I texted Mason:

ETA us vs. plane?

You'll beat plane by 5 minutes. Plane will taxi to private-jet terminal where helipad is.

Any concentration of cop cars there?

Not yet. Will advise if happens.

I put away the phone and looked at my watch. About 15 more minutes. My eyelids were drooping. I wished I could catnap.

The land outside the windows was now almost all brown but spotted with long fingers of green — gully paths down mesas — converging into streams and a river. It looked like fingers of buried green monsters trying to claw their way up out of their graves. I shivered.

Then, up ahead, there was much more green, with a city perched in the middle of it. San Luis Potosí, presumably.

I touched Carmen, pointed ahead, and raised my eyebrows. Her lips started moving into her headset, although I could hear nothing. She stopped, waiting, then nodded her head at me.

I wrote on the paper, "Anything strange? Is he asking the ground for help? People?"

She shook her head no, but then raised her hands and shrugged her shoulders. She didn't think so, but wasn't completely sure.

There could be coded words we'd never know.

I *really* missed my Rugar LC9. I twisted both ankles in my boots, feeling the knife in each ankle holster. Better than nothing. Barely.

A woman with a gun can hold men at bay. A woman with a knife? Even two knives? Not so much. There's a good chance some man will think he can take her. The kind of man who would think himself a coward if he didn't take such a teeny, tiny risk. The kind of man for whom being a coward is the worst thing he can imagine.

The pilot veered left to take us to the northeast section of the town. Soon we saw the small airport there. I looked at Carmen. She again gave me the "I don't think so but can't be sure" combination of head shake and raised hands.

My phone vibrated. I looked quickly.

> Two maybe-armored Jeep Saharas just arrived at your terminal. Drug cartel vehicles??
>
> Jet still 5-6 minutes after you land.

I wrote again on the paper: "Stay behind me. There may be a problem. We have to delay five minutes after we land before our next ride comes." Carmen and Emma both read it and nodded. I crumpled and shoved the paper into my jeans pocket.

The pilot landed and shut down the helicopter. He opened the door and jumped out, then made to help us out.

I held my hands up to stop him, then brought them to my face and covered my eyes. I ran my hands through my hair and tried my best to feel like I was dizzy and nauseous.

"*Uno momento*," I said with a quivering voice.

"Sara, what's wrong?" asked Carmen, with the perfect touch of concern.

"I feel dizzy. A little nauseous. Just give me a minute or two here."

Carmen turned to the pilot and fired off some Spanish. He looked at her, considering, but then fished in his pockets and came out with a hanky.

"*Agua*," she demanded.

The pilot reached back in and handed her a bottle of water. Carmen leaned over the front and opened the other door. She uncapped the water bottle and, leaning outside, poured some over the hanky and squeezed it out. She came back inside, leaving the door open, and put the hanky on my head.

"There, there," she said. "You want water?"

"Just a sip," I managed.

She handed me the bottle. I took a sip and handed it back. I lay back against my seat and held the hanky on my forehead.

"*Gracias*," I said.

The pilot looked at us and said, "Do you need a doctor?" Aha. I thought he might know English.

I shook my head. "I shouldn't. These never last longer than five minutes. Just let me rest here a little longer, and I should be fine.

The pilot stood there, uncomfortable.

I turned to the two women. "You girls get out the other side and stretch your legs. Get some air. Just give me a couple of minutes." The helicopter wouldn't protect against gunfire, so I didn't want them trapped inside. And since my door was facing the terminal, that would give them a little extra distance.

I turned my head and looked out toward the smallish, squat, metal-sided building with yellow paint, apparently used by owners of the private planes parked just 100 yards away and the heliport. Nobody was coming out toward us.

Yet.

It's amazing how long five minutes can take. I laid my head back against the seat and fluttered my eyes — keeping a view of the terminal. Then its door opened, and one man walked out. He was Mexican, medium height, slightly overweight, and dressed in a suit — as if he were airport management. However, the style of the suit and the way it draped on him told me no airport manager could have afforded it. He also strutted like he owned the place.

I looked at the pilot, who didn't recognize the man. But... he recognized the arrogance and it worried him.

The suited man walked up to the helicopter door and looked in at me. "Is there a problem?"

"Oh, señor," I said. "*Lo siento*. I'm sorry if I'm causing problems. I'm just... I feel so dizzy."

I caught movement on the other side of the helicopter and turned. A tiny two-engine jet with "CEO Jets" on the side was landing.

Finally!

I turned back to the two men and took a deep breath. "I will try to get out," I said. The pilot leaned in to help me. The other man hadn't moved an inch. Apparently, he had no reflexive need to help a pitiful woman. Or he knew too much about me to buy my act.

I stood carefully, one hand bracing myself on the helicopter, the other leaning on the pilot. Carmen leaned in and got my bag, then the two women came around to our side.

"I think I can walk," I said tentatively. I leaned harder on the pilot, then let go of the helicopter and took a couple of steps toward the other man and the terminal. Carmen and Emma moved behind me.

Looking past the pilot, I saw the jet taxiing toward us. I took another step toward the other man, then cried out and fell forward, hard on the concrete. I managed to land within three feet of the man, but the creep didn't move a hand to stop my fall.

I knew it would jolt my ribs, so I'd held my breath as I tumbled. But the ribs were mending fast — they didn't hurt any worse than my knee did, slamming to the ground.

The pilot and the two women knelt down beside me. They blocked the other man's view of me, so my right hand closed on one of my boot knives.

"*Lo siento. Lo siento*," I apologized.

The women started to help me up. I did not look at the other man for fear he would see something in my eyes. He was just two feet from me when I rose up with the help of the women. I rose but continued the movement straight to the man. My left arm swung around his neck pulling me into him as if for a kiss. The knife in my right hand went partially into the front of his neck — his trachea. Blood trickled out.

I said, "Touch one of your guns, and I'll bury this knife."

"Okay," he said with a smile, bringing both hands up and grabbing both my arms. I felt pressure as he tried to pull my arms away from him. Amusement disappeared from his face as he tried harder. And harder. Connor might have been able to break my grip. I wasn't sure. But this man was no match for my wolf strength.

"E. Sanchez," I said, using the name tag the pilot wore. "I recommend you get back in your helicopter and stay there for at least 10 minutes. Now!"

"Of course," he said, moving away quickly. I heard the 'copter door close.

"Ladies, get on each side of this gentleman and put your arms around him. We're all one big, happy family, right?"

The man gave a big phony smile as the girls encircled him. "This is fun. Now what?"

Looking over his shoulders, I could see that nobody else had left the terminal.

Yet.

I removed my left hand from his neck and patted him, pulling out a pistol from behind his back. It was an FN Five-SeveN with 20 rounds. Also known as a cop killer.

An engine sounded louder. From the side of my eye, I saw CEO Jets spinning around in a half circle. It ended up pointed back out toward the runway. It was maybe 300 yards from us.

The man's eyes widened as he realized we were heading toward the plane. I could see it dawn on him that we might actually escape. He was a nano-second from doing something really stupid. I removed the knife and slammed his gun right into his neck — hitting the left carotid artery.

"Hold him!" I warned the women as he lost consciousness. We

ran with him, Carmen and I carrying him really, although he was upright and looked from a distance as if he was running with us.

The jet door opened, and steps came down. Carmen and I got him to the top of the steps.

Then I noticed Emma had stopped. She stood there, at the foot of the steps, and looked back toward the terminal.

"They're going to sell you," I told her. "To a man who can do any damn thing he wants with you. He'll pay a fortune for you because he wants to hurt you as long and as bad as he can."

Her eyes widened. "You don't know that."

"The men who came into your room to see you. They were figuring out how much they were willing to pay to own you."

She shook her head. Her eyes looked frantic. Finally, I understood what I should have expected.

"You're addicted to the drugs they gave you. You're jonesing right now without them."

She shook her head no, then yes, then no.

"The man who buys you will love watching you jones. How desperate you'll be."

She shook her head no. Behind her, I saw the doors to the terminal open.

"Damnit, Emma, I've got the proof." I reached into a pocket. "Let me show you." I came down the stairs holding my hand out to her. I walked right up to her and, without even slowing, I punched her in the solar plexus, knocking the air out of her. I'd almost hit her in the jaw, but I didn't need broken knuckles again. I vowed to only punch soft stuff from now on.

I threw her over my shoulder, wincing only a little, and climbed back up the stairs with her. I shoved her at Carmen and said, "Strap her in."

The copilot was standing by the door, his eyebrows raised. His name tag read James Stoffel.

"Hi James," I said, "I hope you have enough fuel left to get us to the U.S."

"No problem."

"Stairs up, door stays open until we get to the runway."

He nodded and raised the stairs.

Six men with rifles were now running toward us. I was pretty sure the guns were automatic or semi-automatic.

I slammed our captive man face down on the floor and pushed his head outside the plane. I pointed his pistol at his head.

"Stop," I yelled. They couldn't hear me. I aimed the pistol far above their heads and pulled the trigger. *That* they heard.

I jammed the pistol against the man's head and yelled again, "Stop, and we'll let him out at the runway."

This time they either heard me or the pistol at their boss' head made my point. The men slowed to a walk, but they kept coming.

"Carmen?" I yelled. "Tell them."

She stuck her head out the door and yelled in Spanish to them. The six men stopped, but two of them raised their guns. I pushed Carmen away from the door and moved my head from view. All they could see was their boss's head and the gun pointing at it.

The jet moved away, and the men followed it. Guns now lowered. The plane gathered speed, outpacing the men. As another plane came in for landing, the men slowed even more. We were now maybe 600 yards from them.

James came back as the plane spun ninety degrees to take off. "We're ready to leave," he said.

"Close the door." I pushed the man out the opening, dropping him to the tarmac. The copilot fastened the door.

"Get us out of here fast. His men have automatic rifles."

The copilot stuck his head into the cockpit, and the plane started moving. Fast.

He came back to my seat as I was buckling in. He nodded his head at Emma, who had awakened. She looked pissed.

"Kidnapping?" he asked.

I shook my head. "A rescue. We'll turn her over to the FBI when we land."

"They're expecting her?"

"Nope. It's a surprise package for them."

He raised his eyebrows and shook his head. But he walked back to the cockpit.

151

The takeoff was too noisy to hear if there were gunshots. As long as we got off the ground — that was enough for me. For now. I was looking forward to some downtime on the plane. I'd been awake for... I looked at my phone. Almost 26 hours. I wanted to decompress. Catch up on my sleep.

Fat chance...

34

Sara Flores
In the air from Mexico to Tulsa

We'd barely reached altitude when Emma started crying. Big, sloppy tears — which were okay — but soon loud wails of despair. I wanted to be empathetic. I really did. I got that she was in pain from withdrawal. But her voice was like fingernails on a blackboard — only much, much louder.

I wanted to punch her again just to shut her up. But I couldn't. To get her into the plane, yes. Because she was annoying the hell out of me — no.

No matter how much I craved it.

Instead, we gave her liquor. That quieted her for, oh, maybe 10 seconds. Then she got angry. She cursed me for forcing her onto the plane. She cussed everyone on the plane out. I was impressed with her vocabulary — I had no idea there were that many things you could say about fornicating with dogs.

Then she got up out of her seat and headed for the pilots — screaming they had to take her back. I grabbed her and threw her back in her seat. I gave her my most intimidating glare, and she looked away. I sat back down and took some deep breaths.

Like a flash, Emma was out of her seat and racing to the cabin door. She grabbed the handle to open it. I ran to her faster than I'd ever run before. I grabbed her, ripped her away from the door, carried her back to her seat, and threw her back in it.

I took out zip ties to fasten her there, and she hit me in the eye with a roundhouse punch.

It hurt! I'd never been hit in an eye before, and I was shocked at the amount of pain. I clenched my fists, then made myself unclench them. I finished zip-tying her to the seat.

She started screaming. I got a rag and jammed it in her mouth. She spit it out.

I ripped off one of the ties that held back the curtains into the pilot cabin, came back, re-jammed the rag in her mouth, and secured it with the curtain tie.

The noise level went down some — but it was still too much. She was shaking her head and body, kicking her feet, and making all the noise she could through the rag.

I walked slowly up to the pilot's cabin, trying to lower my blood pressure. James and the pilot both turned and looked at me, eyebrows raised. Without saying anything out loud, their looks clearly asked, *DO YOU HAVE ANY IDEA WHAT THE FUCK YOU ARE DOING?*

I said, "Please, please, tell me one of you has a sleeping pill you can donate to the cause?"

Fortunately, James did.

How do you give a pill to a kicking, screaming maniac? The same way any pet owner has learned to give one to an unwilling dog or cat.

Her hands were tied so she couldn't punch me again — I was going to have a black eye from her previous lucky shot. I got behind her so she couldn't kick me and undid the gag. Naturally, she started screaming again. I grabbed her jaws and pried them open. She wanted badly to bite me, but really — compared to my wolf-dog Skidi — her jaw strength wasn't much.

I tilted her head back so I could drop the pill as far down her throat as possible, then I slammed her jaws shut and held them up so gravity could work on the pill. Then I pinched her nostrils shut and she panicked — her throat trying to swallow air. Finally, when I was absolutely sure the pill was down, I let go. She tried her best to bring back up the pill, but it didn't work.

When she started screaming again, I reattached the gag.

I walked back up to the pilots and asked if they had an extra set of headphones. I looked back into the cabin, and Carmen was pointing frantically to herself.

"Two sets," I corrected. "If you have them." Amazingly, they did. I walked back and handed one to Carmen.

"*Brava, chica,*" she said to me, laughing her ass off.

I sank down in a seat, pulled on the headphones, and was asleep before I could could count to ten.

35

Sara Flores
Tulsa International Airport

I woke up as we landed in Tulsa. My phone said it was noon, but I sure didn't feel like I got four hours of sleep.

Besides, Judy said the flight was only three and a half hours, and Judy is never wrong.

I removed the headset from my ears and rubbed my eyes. I remembered Emma and glanced to where she was still zip tied. She looked asleep. I unbuckled and walked to the cockpit.

James looked back at me, and I gave him a questioning look and tapped my watch.

He smiled. "Mexico stopped doing daylight savings time," he said.

So I had three hours of sleep.

The jet taxied to the private aircraft terminal, where we couldn't exit the plane until we let a customs agent in here to clear us. As we had two women here without passports, that wasn't happening anytime soon.

James opened our stairs, and two men came up into the plane. One of them was Atticus Snowden, our sometime attorney, and the other one had damn well better be a doctor.

At least I got a little wake-me-up blood pressure jolt, as usual, when Atticus joined us. He looked even more, today, like a young Alan Rickman, as the wind had mussed up his otherwise slicked-down hair.

The doctor was introduced as Trevor Hildebrand. Trevor looked like Archie in the ancient comic strips — bright carrot-top hair, mustache and goatee. His round glasses and high eyebrows made him look astonished.

I told him and Atticus what I knew about Emma, although it wasn't much. Critically, I had no idea what drug or drugs they gave her.

Trevor and I walked back to Emma's seat. She was awake now, moaning and rocking herself back and forth. I removed her gag and the rag from her mouth, then walked away.

Trevor tried to talk with her, but it didn't look like he got a response — she never looked at him. He pulled out a light and shined it in her eyes.

Atticus put an arm on my shoulder. I looked at his smiling face. "You're becoming my most interesting client."

"Glad I can enrich your day," I said grumpily.

He just looked at me, eyes twinkling, the corners of his mouth twitching. Finally I forced a smile.

"You outdid yourself with this one."

I rubbed my hands over my face and started to laugh. Atticus grinned widely, and shook his head at me.

Trevor came back to us, sobering us both up.

"I gave her Naltrexone and Buprenorphine to ease her withdrawal symptoms. She should be lucid in an hour or so. I understand she can't go to a hospital until her name and citizenship are determined?"

Atticus nodded.

"I'll be at my clinic all day today. Bring her to me as soon as you can, and I'll run some tests. She's going to need treatment."

Atticus commandeered the card-playing area in the small plane, where two seats faced backward, two faced forward, and a fancy fake-wood table was between them. I looked at Emma, but she was still out of it. I sat next to Atticus and motioned for Carmen to join us.

"Here's my ground rules," I said. "I'm paying Atticus here to represent you and Emma, but your situations are different. She's probably a U.S. citizen, but you're not. Correct?"

Carmen nodded.

"I have two requirements for him helping you. One is you have to tell him the truth. He'll do whatever he has to do so that legally you are a client and, therefore, what you tell him is confidential. I don't need to know if you committed crimes in Mexico. Or elsewhere. But he does need to know.

"Finally, I need to know — right now — anything you can tell me about women being taken from casinos or elsewhere. I think the man who held you is working with someone up here. I need to find that man."

I looked at her. "Any questions?" She shook her head.

I turned to Atticus. "As I told your office, I've heard good things about the Tulsa FBI Agent-in-Charge Austin Wright. That he's a straight arrow. I'm sure he can get both these women into the U.S., but I don't want him disappearing them into a cell. Or dumping them on a plane back to Mexico after he's grilled them for everything they know. I'm trusting you to protect them."

He nodded.

"Carmen, tell me about the women who were held in that place with you. Where did they come from, and what did they do? Were any of them working at casinos?"

"I need some food — badly," she said.

"You're right. I should have thought about that." I jumped up and went to the cockpit. "Can you order some food for everyone here? Including yourselves?"

"Of course, said James. "What do you prefer?"

"Just make it plenty of protein and caffeine."

I returned to Atticus and Carmen. "Food and caffeine is on the way."

I sat back down and looked at Carmen. Was she stalling? "Now tell me what you know."

"I don't know much," she said. "I never got *El Jefe*'s name. Or the name of any of the men who visited. I only hear their voices. I saw a few of the women."

"The FBI will have a good sketch artist." I turned to Atticus. "See if you can't get me copies of any sketches they do. I or my team may recognize one or more of them."

He cocked an eyebrow at me. "I'm a miracle worker, but getting the FBI to share??"

"Tell them to consider it a favor. Because we're saving their butts by handing them a lead on a major kidnapping ring that — by the way — was operating right under their noses."

Atticus smiled. "If I say that more tactfully, I might be able to get them."

I pulled out my phone and showed her the picture of Alaska Brown. "You're 100% sure none of them was this woman? Have you ever seen her — there or elsewhere?"

She looked again but shook her head. "Never. I'm sorry."

"Okay. Any other details about the girls you did see — other than how they look?"

"Well... we didn't talk much. They had them drugged. But... one girl was from Oklahoma City."

I frowned. "And Alaska was from Tulsa. Emma here says she's from Albuquerque."

"One girl was from Phoenix. I think... yes, another was from Tucson."

"Nobody from Texas? Dallas, Houston, or San Antonio?"

"No, nobody."

"Interesting."

I flipped to another picture — this one of Brittany Rebane. "How about this woman?"

Oh, yeah, she recognized her. Her eyes had dropped to the table. Would she try to lie?

"Yes," Carmen said. "She was kept there for three or four days." There was a pause. Then she added, "I had to make a phone call. Pretend to be her. They told me what to say."

"How many phone calls?"

"Two for her. More for others."

Well... so far, what she said stacked up with what I knew.

I pushed her and got a few more details, but they didn't add anything more that would help me find Alaska. Or the man or men behind this.

I started yawning, and it got so big I thought it might split my face. The three hours I got on the plane weren't nearly enough. I held my hands over my eyes.

I turned to Atticus. "I'm going to get out of here. I need sleep as fast as I can get it. Do your magic with Carmen — which is *not* her real name by the way." She and I looked at each other. She smiled and turned to Atticus, "*Mi nombre es Iliana.*"

He smiled back at her. "Glad to meet you, Iliana."

I turned to Atticus. "When you can talk to Emma, please tell her this for me: She's required to tell you everything she knows, from how and where she was taken to who did it and where they took her. Then she has to tell the FBI however much of that you tell her to. After that — she can do whatever she wants. If she wants to go back to Mexico, I'll pay the plane fare. If she wants drug treatment, I'll pay for that. If she wants you to call her parents, yes to that too. It's completely up to her. You'll advise her, but any decisions are hers. Understood?"

"Yes."

I got up to leave ,and Atticus put out an arm to stop me. "Sara, let me be the first to say the black eye looks dashing on you."

I groaned and left him for the cockpit. "You guys okay on everything? Atticus back there is in charge of what happens next and when the plane will be freed. Neither of you is stuck here, but I suspect your company will want somebody watching the plane. That's up to you."

I grabbed my bag, and they opened the door for me. "Oh," I said to the pilots. "I almost forgot. That was some superior flying. Thanks for saving our asses."

They both grinned. The pilot said, "It made me feel like I was back flying in Iraq." Then he grinned wider. "But I'm not much for nostalgia, so next time maybe ask for a different pilot?"

I grinned back. "Oh no," I said, shaking my head and looking at his name tag. "Now that I know how good you two are under stress,

George Crespo and James Stoffel, I plan to ask for you both every time."

Both men gave me those automatic smiles that show you're being a good sport when you don't mean it for a second.

I walked down the stairs and looked around for the food delivery, but unfortunately, it wasn't here yet.

As I walked to the terminal, I called Mason.

"Bad news," he said. "Connor has disappeared."

36

Connor Rockwood
Location unknown

Son-of-a-bitch!
 Connor sat up from the thin, puke-smelling mattress he was lying on. His head felt dizzy, his mouth felt like he'd swallowed a Fallujah sandstorm, and he was in a concrete cell with one air vent and one caged light 12 feet above his head.

He saw thick chains attached to the wall, holding up the outside corners of the metal slab the mattress lay on. He lowered his head between his legs and saw two huge steel hinges attaching the back end of the metal slab to the wall.

There were only two other things in the cell — a hole in the floor and a Lowes 5-gallon paint bucket beside it, filled with water.

How could he have let his guard down like that?

But he knew. Plain, old-fashioned greed did it. He was blinded by all the dollar signs dangled by Winston Bainbridge III. All those casinos. All those threat assessments.

How did he... Connor ran through everything. The meeting, the card, the call from Bainbridge, "Call me Winston."

"I'm taking my jet back to Phoenix," the man had said. "Why not fly down with me? We can talk on the plane, and you can get your first look at our Phoenix flagship. It's the casino I'm most worried about now that you figured out the problem at Tulsa."

Of course. Why not. But since the plane was the last thing he remembered, it had to have happened there. He thought harder. He hadn't been touched by anyone. He hadn't even shaken hands as Winston had already been buckled in. It had to be the vodka.

Once they'd reached altitude, Winston had offered him a boilermaker — surprising Connor that Winston knew his favorite drink. Feeling a little paranoid, Connor had asked instead for a shot of vodka.

"I'll join you," Winston had said, taking out a bottle with glass pinstripes that looked like it might be one of those $1,000+ bottles Connor had heard about and pouring a glass for each of them. It hadn't tasted different to Connor from any other vodka, but then he wasn't a vodka man.

Winston must have had some coating on the glass he poured it in — so whatever Connor asked for would still do the trick.

Oh, god. Sara will never let him hear the end of this. She'd warned him of a sneak attack, and he'd thought he'd protected himself. But apparently, he didn't think sneakily enough.

Hell, he hated sneaky. He preferred break-down-the-door, guns blazing, send-'em-all-to-hell and let the devil sort them out.

'Course, Sara can't rag on him until after he's out of this mess. Which he will be.

He patted his pockets and ankles. His guns and knife were all gone. He crossed his leg and leaned over his body in case there was a camera somewhere. He twisted the boot heel, only to reveal an empty chamber where his emergency communication device should have been.

His belt was missing. *Damn.* He had a great little knife concealed in the belt buckle. He could get another in two days from Amazon, one day even, but that wouldn't help him now.

He stood up and had to brace himself against a wall. What drug had they used on him? But it was wearing off. Connor could feel it loosening its grip.

The door was the only spot in the room that wasn't made of concrete block, so he walked to it. A small window showed only a concrete hall. Nobody there. There was a narrow slot at the bottom of the door where a food tray could come through. He tapped the door — it was steel. He looked at the edges of the door, but he didn't see any hinges. They must be on the outside.

He took off one boot and slammed the heel of it into the glass of the window — to no effect. It had to be bullet resistant, with layers of glass and plastic. Unfortunately, they'd taken his ring — which had a center-placed sharp-point diamond that might have gone through a few of the layers.

He looked down at his shirt. He was reduced to his very last, most paranoid trick. His shirt buttons were attached with a thin wire, not thread. An operator he once worked with taught him that. As well as how to use the wire to pick locks. And how to twist the wires together for something stronger.

There was no lock to pick on the inside of this door, but he might need it later.

Connor started searching to his right, running his hands and eyes along the entire wall — searching for cameras. He took his time and searched every inch he could reach. Nothing there. If they did have cameras, and he had to assume they did, they were at least eight feet high. That meant he could block their view if the time came.

Connor sat back on the bed. They would come for him. He would find his chance then.

But... he felt the lack of not having a team of operators behind him. The security of knowing they would come for him.

What did he have here — with this new group? There was Judy. She was a great logistics guy. Gal. But that wasn't what he needed now. There was Mason. He was undoubtedly looking for Connor right now. And he was good — he would probably find him if he had enough time.

That left Sara, who was more the management type. She had the big picture, figured out the angles, and assigned the tasks.

Or... was that fair? She *had* rescued Judy. She'd taken out two guys to do it, although not both at the same time. Using a gun.

Connor had never been on a mission with a female operative. He'd talked to one guy who had, and the guy said she held her own. But the idea of waiting to be rescued by a woman...

Not a chance in hell. Connor was on his own, and he'd rescue his own damned self.

He lay back on the mattress, deciding to get some shuteye.

Then he froze. Why did Bainbridge leave him alive? It would be so much simpler to disappear him. If he was alive because they wanted intel from him, why weren't they already asking him questions? Why was he left lying here, cooling his heels?

Unless they were expecting Sara to come after him.

Oh shit.

37

Sara Flores
Near Three Points, Arizona

It had taken Judy an hour to get me a flight with a different charter jet company, just in case whoever was watching us was also watching the charter firm we normally used.

That gave me time to rush home, stock up on weapons and a few extra goodies, and take a cab to the Richard Lloyd Jones airport on the south side of Tulsa — anything to sow confusion in the enemy.

This was a smaller jet than we'd had from Mexico — eight rows of two seats a row. I checked, reassuring myself it had two engines. Call me paranoid, but I wasn't getting in anything with just one.

When you can recover from wounds that would kill anyone else, you get much more nervous about what's left that could kill you. Like falling from the sky.

As I buckled in and relaxed the seat back, I saw a Fed Ex van rush up to us and hand off a package. The copilot brought it back to me, told me to raise my seatback (dammit!), and went back to the cockpit for takeoff.

I opened the package as the jets blasted us into the air. My heart dropped when I saw what was inside.

As soon as the pilot allowed, I called Mason.

"What the hell is this you sent me?"

He made a funny squelched noise.

I said, "You'd better not be laughing at me."

"I would never even consider it," he said, sounding strangled. Then he burst out laughing.

"Mason..." I hated the sound of my voice — I was actually whining. "Mason, this is a drone. I don't know how to work a drone. Tell me you're already on a plane to join me."

"This isn't any drone, Sara — this is a Drone-For-Dummies. It's ranked as one of the easiest for complete beginners."

"Complete beginners aren't buying drones — only techies are. A complete beginner techie is way more advanced than a normal human."

"Ouch. But... you need it. Here's why."

Mason had done his tech magic. He'd found Connor getting on a private jet owned by Bainbridge Casinos. The plane first stopped at Ryan Airfield, outside of Tucson, then flew to its home base in Phoenix. Mason couldn't find what happened at Ryan Airfield but he got eyes on the plane in Phoenix. Winston Bainbridge departed there with a single pilot. Nobody else was on board.

Unless they tossed Connor off the plane while in flight — *please, God, no!* — Connor must have exited at Ryan Airfield.

Mason had searched all the business databases for Bainbridge Casinos, plus Winston's personal records. Buried under layers of subterfuge, he found Winston owned a small import/export company with a warehouse outside of Three Points, AZ.

Nearest airport? Ryan Airfield.

"The problem is — the warehouse is sitting on 40 desert acres with no hiding places. You need that drone to see what you'll be facing."

"Mason..."

"Suck it up Sara. Open the box. Look for a "Quick Start Guide."

Sullenly, resentfully, I found the flyer and opened it.

"Great," I said. "Only the title is in English. The rest is in Chinese, Korean... I see Arabic, Turkish, Greek, Russian... oh, and French."

Finally, I found the English. "It's one sentence. 'Check battery level: press once. Power on/off, then press and hold.' That's all the English on the whole damn paper."

"Aren't there drawings?"

I closed my eyes. "You can't mean I have to read technical drawings."

"Well...," he said. "If you really can't, I can get Judy on the phone with you. She figured it out and got one set up in 15 minutes."

"She what?"

He made that strangled sound again, and I hung up.

I wasn't going to admit that I couldn't understand something Judy got in 15 minutes. I'm not proud of how competitive I suddenly felt. But the woman did so many things so well, I was getting a complex. If she could get it in 15 minutes, surely I could get it in the two hours before we landed. Couldn't I?

I scanned one of those code thingies into my phone and double-clicked to install the app. The next picture showed me how to plug it in. Okay, I managed that. It did come in a cute little carrying bag.

There were idiot-proof little stickers on the folded-up drone showing me where to plug it in. But then the little flyer for the "Two-Way Charging Hub" said to first read the manual before using it.

The manual turned out to be 51 pages. Judy did *not* read the whole manual — not in 15 minutes.

I found little plugs that go into a car for the battery charger, so I didn't have to solve it all now. I decided to nap while the drone was starting to charge. I texted Mason:

> Taking a needed nap. Don't bug me until plane is down.

Me? Passive aggressive?

I fell asleep almost the second I reclined the seat.

We landed at Ryan Airfield, just southwest of Tucson, two and a half hours later. A rental jeep was waiting for me, again thanks to Judy. And it had the necessary USB ports.

Judy made my job easier. Too bad I'd have to lose her after this case was solved. But it was that putting-her-in-mortal-danger part — I didn't want that responsibility.

They could have — probably would have — killed her.

I drove west — out into nothing. I passed a clump of trees, but mostly the land was red-tinged desert. The kind of land the U.S. long ago "gave" to indigenous tribes as it stole their more fertile land. Miles and miles of parched earth and small plants gasping for a drop of water.

However, according to a packet from Judy — more help! — that I downloaded on the plane, a trail-of-tears type march hadn't happened here. The Tohono o'Odham, whose land started just west of Three Points, had been here for thousands of years.

I got a jolt of interest when I learned the tribe's territory spread into Mexico as well as the U.S., thinking that might be a worst-case escape route. But, apparently, the border was a nightmare for the tribe. U.S. customs constantly stopped them from moving across to see family or to visit sites important to their religion.

I stopped in Three Points, Arizona, the biggest town for the next two and a half hours of desert driving — before the Ajo so-called "highway" found its way back to civilization. If you went southwest instead, Three Points was 35 miles from Sells, from which a 30-mile trek over roadless terrain would have you at the Mexican border.

The population of Three Points was listed at 4,500 — enough to support a border patrol station, one restaurant, a school and a feed store. Plus an Ace Hardware and the Three Points General Store — where I pulled in, gassed up, and then parked.

I didn't like the entrance to the General Store — it had wide barred gates. Even though both were swung open, they still looked too much like the bars of a cage. My wolf hated it and I agreed. And I worried Connor was behind bars like this right now.

Waiting.

The store offered typical fast food, hot dogs cooking on rollers, candy, soda, etc. Plus a large selection of beer, wine and clothing. A nice assortment of cowboy hats for those who'd just lost one to the wind.

I stocked up with 24 water bottles and several packages of beef jerky — in case of emergency. Then I popped two beef burritos in the microwave and bought a liter of Diet Coke. And, what the hell, some Reese's Cups.

Then I took my booty to the Jeep and pulled to the farthest side of the parking lot — where nobody else was parked.

I swallowed one burrito in two bites, then pulled out the hated drone and looked at the 51-fucking-page manual on my phone.

Fifteen minutes my ass.

I plugged the battery charger into the car and unfolded the drone. It had a snap to detach the incredibly fragile blades for flying. Maybe they'd break instantly, and I would be spared trying to make it work?

More tabs told me to "remove the gimbal protector before taking off." I removed the plastic cap and assumed the "gimbal" was the bouncy thing beneath it. I also peeled off any sticky tabs I could find. Two arms opened out, but the other two were stuck.

Swearing, I put it on the seat beside me and drove toward the warehouse. I stopped when my phone GPS said I was five miles away. The manual said the DJI Mini 2 could go 10 kilometers (a little over six miles) before I would lose the signal.

I pulled over to the side of the road and called Mason.

"I hate you," were my first words to him. "I got it only part way set up, and it's about to get dark. We have maybe an hour of light left. And, by the way, I hate, hate, *hate* feeling this stupid."

Amazingly, he gave me no grief. "Let me see where you're at."

We FaceTimed and I turned off my brain. Mason told me the steps to pop in a battery, and I did it. He told me how to sync it to my phone for visuals, and I did it. Although... I did want to choke him when I realized the drone could come with a video screen built into the controls instead of having to sync up to my phone.

Seeing my scowl, Mason said, "We tried to get the screen console for you. They didn't have one they could get fast enough to make your plane."

Finally, he had the damn thing working. And I managed to fly it around without crashing it.

We popped a fresh battery in it and sent it off to the warehouse.

The visual showed the building, a black van and two late-model pickup trucks parked outside. No people were visible.

"I don't like it," Mason said on the phone.

"You never like it."

"They could have 12 people in there."

"For what — to hold one man? Who had to be incapacitated — or they'd never have gotten him off the plane. This isn't a working warehouse, Mason. Employees aren't showing up here daily and working. This is a store-something-until-you-need-it warehouse."

"Maybe that's how they want it to look. Maybe they're waiting for you to walk into their trap."

"If so, there's probably three men in there — max."

"There could be a lot more."

"Mason," I said. "You forget I'm just a girl. Men never worry about taking me down — that's my superpower. Well... that and my wolf."

"At least tell me you're waiting until night."

"Of course. Because I could be wrong."

38

Sara Flores
Arizona desert outside of Three Points

There was no human way to sneak up on the warehouse. No shrubbery to hide behind — unless you were six inches high. No hills and valleys once you got within visual distance of the place.

I had to assume they had one or more types of perimeter protection in addition to any guards. Probably not buried mines, but likely radar and almost certainly infrared.

Connor was probably there, and they might be torturing him for information. This was my worst nightmare with involving other people. I sweated it all the time with Mason. Now I had two more to worry about.

Because it was my fault Connor was probably in there.

We had no excuse to bring in cops or the feds. And a full-frontal assault — assuming we had the people, which we didn't — would be bad tactics. They could easily kill him before we could get to him.

I'd known what I was going to do almost from the first. I was going to lope around the grounds in wolf form, as if I were hunting rabbits. If they had rabbits around here? Well, they had something small and edible for wolves to snack on.

No perimeter detection system was set up to send in the calvary for a lone animal on the grounds.

They had coyotes here, I could hear their barks in the distance. But southwest coyotes topped out at 25 pounds. There could be some Mexican wolves here — a few packs have been seen in Arizona and New Mexico. That species of wolf tops out at 80 pounds.

My wolf is 130 pounds — much larger than any local wolves. I figured if I loped along, it would be clearest to radar and infrared that I'm a 4-legged creature. That should tell them — even given my size — that I'm absolutely no threat to them.

Until I am.

I pulled out my backpack that's configured so I can wear it when I'm in wolf form. It contained a throw-away .38 automatic I got from a very bad man last year who no longer needed it because he was no longer alive. I'd packed three extra magazines for it and thrown in two bottles of water and four packs of beef jerky. Plus a t-shirt and shorts. I also attached a com link to Mason on the outside of the bag. We double-checked that it was working.

Normally I wear the pack on my back, but the radar might show something that would have them questioning what I was. I figured I'd let it hang down across my chest and stomach. Depending on how good their systems are, maybe they'll think I'm a pregnant wolf.

The last light faded from the sky — leaving it black velvet, studded with rhinestone stars everywhere. More than I ever saw in Oklahoma, because there were no lights out here to hide them. Rhinestones from one horizon to the other — enough even for one of those capes Elvis used to wear at the end when he used their flash to make up for the hot young body he no longer had.

No moon yet, which I regretted. Transforming is excruciatingly painful — made slightly better if the moon is out. The pull of the moon can distract you a little, at least at the start.

I laid out the backpack so my wolf could easily slip into it. I realized I was stalling. I scrunched up my face. If I could have pounded my head against a wall, I would have.

I *hate* this!

Don't get me wrong — I love being a wolf. And the transformation lasts just one minute — so you might think I have a lot of nerve complaining. But that's because you haven't spent 60 very, very long seconds wishing to hell you could die — instantly. I can't even scream in pain near the end because my voice box doesn't work then.

Shit. Shit. Shit!

Think of Connor, I told myself. And I did.

I undressed. Then I took a deep breath and opened myself up to the change. It's not so much that I *make* it happen. It's more that I *allow* it to happen.

And it hurt every bit as much as I remembered.

It starts with my hands, fingernails ripping themselves out and turning into claws. Then my toes. Fur starts rippling out on my arms and legs.

Next — it feels like all my teeth are jerked out at once by a dentist. Followed by sharp — bigger — fangs forcing their way out of my tender, bleeding gums. And — just for giggles — an extra 10 teeth break through the gums. Which they have room to do because my nose has melded to my upper lip, and both of them have moved forward a good 8 inches.

And that's just the opening act.

I think it's a survival mechanism for werewolves that your voice box stops working just as the even worse pain starts. You really don't want to know what it feels like when your knees suddenly bend backward. Or when, for a grand finale, your spine cracks and bends the opposite direction from a human spine.

I lay there on the ground a few seconds, so relieved that the pain was over.

Finally, I got up on my four legs, slipped my front paws and my head through the backpack straps, shrugged it into as comfortable a place as it would get, and started trotting to the warehouse.

And here's the funny part — I feel spectacular when I'm a wolf. Better than I've ever felt as a human. I feel high as if I've inhaled some magic fairy dust. Really, I want to giggle it feels so good.

In wolf form, I feel like I belong — like I'm an integral part of the world.

All that human angst of wondering what the meaning of life is — all gone. Life just is. Life is something you savor — as long as you have it. Someday — poof — it'll be gone. But while you have it — you revel in the fullness of it. You love. You fight. You support your pack. Play with puppies. Use your brains to find better food sources. Better dens. Lay in the sun. Chase rabbits.

It's all so freaking wonderful!

I didn't need any night vision goggles — I saw clearly ahead — the brush, the small hills.

I wanted to tear into a run — leaping and rolling and laughing at the night. Instead, I forced myself into a wolf trot. That easy, loping, one-with-nature, eat-up-the-ground, four-mph speed that I could keep up for as many hours as I wanted. The movement felt as natural as sitting on my ass does as a human.

Soon the warehouse came into view. I made myself stop occasionally and sniff the ground. Pretend to sniff for rabbits. There weren't any here. But I sniffed out several ground squirrels. They'd normally be out foraging in the night, but these had smelled me or felt the light thump of my paws on the earth and were now quaking as deep in their holes as they could hide.

When I was about 50 feet from the warehouse, I slowed my trot to a stroll. A wolf would be cautious about a place where humans could be. Wolves are neophobic — they're afraid of new things. It's the only reason they survived after humans tried their damn best to wipe them out.

I strolled closer and found cigarette butts around the door — carrying the smell of two different men. The moisture of your mouth sucking on a cigarette holds your odor for a little while.

I moved around back and found the scent where three men had peed. One was the same man as one of the smokers, but two were new. That meant at least four men were inside.

Plus, hopefully, Connor — even though his smell was not here.

I wanted to enjoy the full bouquet of pee smells, but I didn't have the time.

I tried once to explain to Mason how fascinating the smells were. How you could peel back one layer after another of surprises about a person — their health, what they eat, when they last had sex, even hints about their personality.

What a mistake. To this day, Mason gives me grief about it.

I moved over to the van and two trucks and inhaled the smells. Another unknown-man smell came from one of the trucks — that made at least five. And — yes! — Connor's smell came from the side of the van. No fear or anger to the smell — he was probably unconscious. But he was here. Thank God.

I strolled back to the entrance door and stood there. I knew their sensors had spotted me. I figured some yahoo would eventually come out — if only to shoot me for "fun." Sure enough, after a couple of minutes I heard the inside locks retract.

Since I didn't want the "fun" of being shot, I moved to the side of the door and flattened myself against the wall. A rifle barrel proceeded the man out, so I had a good idea exactly where he was. I launched myself for his throat, opened my jaws, and bit his head mostly off before he could make a sound. It was good I went for the throat — he was wearing body armor.

Did I feel guilty? No. This group was trafficking women and was killing people to protect themselves. They'd attacked Judy, and now they had Connor. If I didn't succeed here, Connor would be dead.

I was grateful to have one man down — knowing there were at least four more. Maybe quite a few more, despite what I had told Mason.

I was covered in blood from my snout to my front paws, including the front of my backpack. I was going to leave a trail. I needed to clear the building so I could protect against anyone coming up behind me. I sunk my teeth into his bulletproof vest and easily dragged his body back inside the building. I let the door close.

I faced a very long hallway with four doors opening on the sides before it ended in a larger room. The first two doors were both open, and the rooms were empty. The third door in the hallway was closed. I stood up on my hind legs, my body to the side of the door in case someone wanted to spray bullets through it. I pressed my front foot pads against the doorknob and tried to turn it. Right then left. The latch opened and I pushed the door in, staying back against the wall.

Nobody shot at me. I looked inside and found this room, too, was empty.

I struck out with the room across from it. The knob wouldn't turn. The door was locked. I didn't smell anyone inside, but I might not. I was leaving danger behind me.

Ahead the hallway spilled out into a wider area. I saw two tables, each surrounded with empty metal chairs. Inhaling, I smelled two men whose scent I recognized off to the right from where I stood.

Carefully, I smelled the air — checking for anyone else. A surprise could be deadly. For me and for Connor.

I risked darting my head around the wall and quickly back. The men were playing cards. The good news was no guns were lying on the table — requiring only seconds to use. I was sure they had guns, but they were in holsters or — if rifles — propped against one of the walls. The bad news? They were on opposite sides of the table. I couldn't lunge and knock over both at once.

The idea of reducing bad-guy numbers to just two excited me. But I had to warn myself that there could be more than the five I expected.

The closest man was about 15 feet from me. I can leap only 12-13 feet. (Of course I tested it. Wouldn't you?) So... I was going to have to take one stride and then leap. More time required — during which I could be shot.

177

39

Sara Flores
Warehouse outside of Three Points, Arizona

I bunched my hind leg muscles and sped into the room. I took that one step, then launched myself at the closest man — open mouth and aiming for the throat. I hit him hard and we went to the floor. He'd got a hand up in front of it to block me, but that was no problem for the strength of my jaws. His hand and his throat were useless by the time we hit the floor.

Quickly I turned and stuck my nose under the metal table. I shoved my end up into the air and hit the second man with it just as he drew his gun. He fired twice right before the table landed on him, both bullets leaving round holes in the table far too close to where my head had been.

Worried about the noise bringing more men, I quickly nosed under the table to get at him.

He slammed the gun against my head — disorienting me for a second. I watched, fascinated, as the gun muzzle turned toward me.

It appeared to move in slow motion.

It was almost pointed at my head before I could shake myself into action. Again I went for the throat — tearing out his trachea and one or both of his carotid arteries. Whatever — there was blood everywhere.

My ears picked up a door opening, and I froze.

I heard footsteps coming closer to us.

Quietly, I lay there on top of the last man — both of us partially under the table.

Playing dead.

I kept my mouth closed so the newcomer wouldn't see blood on my teeth.

"What the hell?"

Bad training, I thought. Connor wouldn't have blurted out anything like that. You walk into a blood-bath scene, you pull out your weapons, and you keep absolutely quiet. Nobody human would have known he was there if he hadn't talked. I only knew thanks to my wolf ears.

And, now, I could also smell him. He was stinking of fear.

My nose told me it was only one man. I used it and my ears to guesstimate exactly where he was standing.

I was probably going to get shot. I accepted that. What I most needed to avoid was a headshot or multiple shots.

I kept my eyes closed, my ears facing him, and my nose on full alert.

He was closer now. Maybe 15 feet.

Then closer.

I felt the table move a little. He was likely toeing it with his boot.

"What the hell?" This time his voice was softer. Questioning.

I felt the table lifted up off me and the man I was lying on. I kept my eyes closed and stopped breathing.

Something metal jostled my body. The point of his rifle?

He was as close as he was likely to get.

I couldn't leap at the man — not from a lying-flat position. So I swung my head and reached as far as I could and got my jaws around his right forearm. I bit it off, and the rifle dropped.

Unfortunately, the man had some training.

Instead of grabbing his stump, his left hand grabbed a .44 from a side holster, pulled it out, and shot me just as I was getting my legs under me.

He pulled the trigger twice, sending searing agony into my chest.

Assuming I'd been taken care of, he then dropped his gun, ripped his shirt and started making a tourniquet for his right arm.

It wasn't my heart. I was grateful for that. But my lungs were leaking oxygen and I started gasping for air. The pain in my chest was almost as bad as transforming.

While he was struggling with just one arm to make the tourniquet, I got up and used my jaws to grab his .44 off the floor.

His eyes looked at me in disbelief.

I forced myself to carry it — staggering — back into the hallway where I dropped it. Then I went back and carried away his rifle.

I fell to the floor in the hall where he couldn't see me. Normally I have to eat meat to force the transformation back to human. But a really serious injury will also do the trick. Like my bullet-ridden lungs that were leaking air that I needed to breathe. I lay there and willed the transformation to take me back to human. Quickly, please? Please?

Anything to stop the pain.

But no matter how I begged, it took the full 60 seconds.

Finally, I lay there in human form. I gulped all the air I could into my lungs. Just to be extra sure, I felt my chest — no bullet holes. No bleeding. I could breathe freely and deeply.

What an amazing thing that is — getting oxygen into your body.

What a miracle Joe White Wolf gave me when he turned me. I'd been a coward of a woman before — always running from trouble. The only reason I had courage now was because I knew I could survive gunshots. Although — was it really courage when I had that knowledge?

I shook my head. No time for philosophy. No time to get dressed. I needed to see right this second how far along he'd gotten.

I picked up the rifle and walked back into the room — human and naked except for a few splotches of blood from where I had lain.

The man had finished his makeshift tourniquet, but he was pale with the loss of blood.

His eyes widened when he saw me — I must have been quite a sight.

He reached down with his good hand and pulled a .38 automatic off his ankle.

My first instinct was to shoot him. Anyone else here had probably already heard the previous gunshots. Probably.

But just in case... The moment he moved, I ran toward him, landing on him, grabbing him — smashing his hand with the gun between us so he couldn't fire.

I wrapped my arms and legs tightly around him, holding us together. His other arm with the tourniquet ended up right in front of my face. I grabbed the cloth with my human teeth and jerked as hard as I could. It slipped down his arm and came off his stump — letting loose all the blood he'd been holding back.

He jerked and head-butted me, but I held on tight. His jerks got slower and more feeble.

It didn't take long. He was unconscious in 20 seconds and his heart stopped pumping about a minute later.

Four men down. At least one — maybe more — to go. And I still had to find Connor.

I found some paper towels in the kitchenette and wiped the blood off my face and body as well as I could. Then I found my backpack and pulled on my t-shirt and shorts. I stuck my throwaway .38 automatic in the back of my waistband. Then I gathered up two of the rifles in the room and swung them over my left shoulder.

I took the dead guy's .44 and let it lead the way as I searched the rest of the floor. I found nobody. But I did find stairs leading down a level.

I held all my weapons tight against my body to keep from making any noise. My bare feet were silent as a wolf.

Once I went down two steps, I could smell a new man. Not one of the five I'd smelled outside.

Damn! That meant there were at least six men here. Four dead and one down these stairs. But where was the other?

I winced. I hadn't cleared that locked room upstairs. But surely I'd have smelled anyone in there?

Wherever he was, he'd be able to find me easy enough — my bare feet were leaving bloody footprints to guide him.

I reached the last step before the stairway turned. Before the man would be able to see me. I quietly hooked my little finger on my left hand through the trigger guard of the .44 and let it dangle. I wanted it close. The rifles should be more accurate, but I didn't know how many shells each carried, and — stupid me — I hadn't checked before coming down here.

I knew next to nothing about rifles — I'd never trained with them. Another hole in my education I'd been hoping Connor could plug for me.

I shouldered one of the rifles and looked down the sights. I edged the rifle tip and my eye around the corner at the same time.

There was a hallway with four cells leading off of it. A folding chair was beside one of the cell doors. It was empty.

The man who'd been sitting in it was up and pacing — his back to me for this instant. His hands were twitching — including the one holding a .44. He was arguing with himself.

He turned back, part of his pacing, and his eyes widened at the sight of me.

"Drop the gun," I said, willing to give him a chance. I'd lock him in the cell instead of Connor.

Instead, he brought it up and pointed it at me. He was just a little too slow. His shot hit the ceiling as his face disappeared from my shot. I was shocked. I'd been aiming at his heart. I really *did* need to train with rifles.

Quickly I looked behind me. No sixth man. Not yet, at least.

I looked in each of the cells. Nobody was visible in any of them. Three of them opened without a key and were empty.

I pawed the dead guard until I found the keys, and unlocked the fourth cell and stood back.

"Connor? It's Sara."

Nothing happened for a second, then Connor's head came into view. Quickly he looked outside the cell and saw the dead guard. He looked back at me. He sped to the guard and took the man's .44, checking the mag to see how many bullets were left.

I handed him one of the rifles.

"Nice uniform," he said to me.

I looked down at my blood-spotted shorts and bloody bare feet. "I like to be comfortable," I said.

I took a better look at him. No bruises. Nothing looked hurt. But he was wearing a dress shirt which was missing every single button.

"They removed each of your buttons?"

"I did." He held out his left hand and I saw a many-strand wire long enough for a garrote and sharp enough on one end to maybe pick a lock.

"Nice trick," I said. "You have to teach me that."

Then I remembered.

"There's at least one man not accounted for," I told him. "Let's try to get out of here."

We came back up the stairs, and Connor saw the mess in the kitchen area. He walked over to look while I busted into the room with the locked door but nobody was inside. And even my human nose could tell nobody had been in there recently.

I came out and turned my head, trying to smell the missing man — but my human nose was getting nothing.

"Three men?" he asked.

I knew what he was asking. "Not at the same time. Two — then one."

He had a funny look on his face as he took in the ripped throats and a missing arm.

"A little blood-thirsty, aren't you?"

I shrugged. "Cross me, and I become an animal."

I picked up my backpack, reached inside, and pulled out the camera pin and earpiece. I removed the mic from where it was pinned on the outside of the bag. I put it all on and tapped the mike.

"We're both safe," I told Mason. "Although we're missing one bad guy."

There was a very long silence, then I heard Mason say, "I never doubted it."

"Liar," I said, smiling. I loved how he always worried about me. "We need to find any cameras they have here."

I turned to Connor. "I want to burn this place. Can you prep that? Also..." I pointed toward the door. "I came in that way. So it's clear for about 90 degrees. If the sixth man is outside and a sniper, he'll be somewhere between here and here." I indicated the 270-degree possibilities.

"How do you know there's a missing man?"

"I smelled him."

Connor gave me a look.

"Was I right about the cocaine?"

He nodded. "Okay, okay."

I tapped my earpiece again. "Mason, what do I do to find the cameras?"

Mason guided me, unerringly, to the cameras and then to the computer running them. Then he told me to do one thing after another, almost none of which I understood. But, hey, I do know how to follow directions.

No matter what some people might say.

At one point, Mason got very excited and started babbling about "hack back" and "blow back" and a bunch of other terms that might as well be Sanskrit for all I understood them.

Finally, he finished ordering me around.

I went back to take pictures and fingerprints of each dead body. Then I found Connor, and together we torched the place. We walked out to the vehicles with me staring out where a sniper might be waiting. We split up to figure out which truck to take.

Too late, I noticed that the three vehicles had multiplied into four — an extra truck was parked here, sitting innocently among the others.

Oh crap!

Before I could yell a warning to Connor, I heard the cocking of a rifle behind me.

I prayed it wasn't aimed at my head. Maybe I could transform and survive a shot to the head, but I don't know and I sure as hell never want to find out.

I threw myself flat to the ground as the rifle fired. I rolled and turned, and brought up my .44 and pointed it toward where the man had to be.

Halfway through my instinctive moves, I had a fleeting wonder why there was no pain. Just before I would have fired in return, I wondered why the man was collapsing in on himself and headed for the ground, the rifle falling from his hands.

Then I saw the blooming red stain at the man's heart.

I looked around and saw Connor come out from behind a truck, putting up his rifle, smugness in his eyes. He came forward and reached out a hand to me.

I grabbed it and rose to my feet.

"Damnit, Flores," he said, "I can't keep saving you like this. You need to pull your own weight."

I smirked. "You're right. I'll try to keep up."

40

Sara Flores
Sara's office in Tulsa

It was a relief to be back in my Tulsa office after a luxurious eight hours of sleep. I smiled at my reject coffee table and chairs. I even patted my crappy desk.

It was even more of a relief to finally know who we were up against in this case. Winston Bainbridge III. The billionaire who'd both grabbed Connor and was running this whole female trafficking operation.

I called Mason to see how he was doing with the electronic files we'd found in the warehouse — the files that lead directly to Bainbridge. Mason was doing something magical with them — using them to get into Bainbridge's files elsewhere. He'd been on it for the past 24 hours.

"Go away, Sara," he'd almost growled. I'd never heard him like this. "Don't call me again unless the world is ending. I'll call you when I'm done."

"But..."

"Go away. For at least a day."

He hung up on me.

Well, hell.

I pictured a day of going crazy, pacing back and forth, and decided instead to go check out our new Wichita safe house. At home, I packed a small bag and then, with a grin, loaded Skidi into the truck. I could at least have the fun of seeing how Judy's cat reacts to a half-wolf. And vice versa.

On the road, I checked in with Connor. He was hanging out at a buddy's fishing cabin. When I expressed worry, he told me they had enough weapons there to take over a small country. And his friend was *almost* as good as he was.

There was a "thunk" as the phone must have been dropped. He picked it back up, said, "Sorry," and dissolved in laughter. He was joined by more laughter in the background. I was relieved he had at least one good friend there to watch his back.

He was probably safe enough. For a day or two.

GPS delivered me to our new Wichita address, but when the complex revealed itself, I froze and gawked — long enough to hear a horn demanding I move along.

There had to be 14 separate four-story buildings spread out along the riverside and interconnected to a main area. Tenant parking was under the buildings but not underground — so you could see the full football-field length and width of it.

Yes, I understood the logic of an upscale, gated apartment complex. It was large enough to not have people watching your every move and was protected from easy penetration. However... seeing it was different. Seeing it felt like I was becoming some yuppie or yuccie or whatever. Pretentious.

I sighed. Things were changing too fast. I was on a runaway train. Half of me liked it, and the other half wanted to jump off right this second.

I managed to find our two parking slots, then grabbed my bag. I held out the leash for Skidi. She gave me her look that said both, "You've got to be kidding" and "You know I could break this with one chomp if I wanted to."

"I know, I know," I told her. "It's so kind of you to humor me."

We got in the elevator with a couple who scooted back as far as they could — giving Skidi maximum room.

"She's really very sweet," I told them.

They nodded distractedly, but their eyes never left her. They darted out on the second floor, relief written all over their faces.

Judy greeted me at the door and, after a second's hesitation, patted Skidi. I felt a jolt of guilt as I saw the blue metal splint on her index finger.

I dumped my bag in the second bedroom and let her show me around. She pointed out all the amenities and the security upgrades Mason had done — talking nonstop.

I oohed and aahed, but my eyes kept coming back to her finger. Finally, I couldn't take it.

"Judy," I said. She stopped and looked at me.

"Just come here for a second." I opened my arms.

Looking puzzled, she came to me. I wrapped my arms around her and and squeezed.

"I'm just so glad you're safe," I said. "The last time I saw you a masked man was carrying your limp body out of your apartment."

"Oh," she said. "Well, aren't you sweet."

"Sweet?" I was horrified. "If you tell anyone I'm 'sweet,' I'll... I'll..."

She patted my back. "Don't worry, I'll never tell."

I sat down on the sofa. Skidi came over and buried her head in my lap.

Judy said, "Nobody would believe me, anyway."

I brushed it off. "You just scared me, that's all. I'm happy to see you doing great." I took a breath and changed the subject.

"I love what you did with the place." I waved my hands at the apartment.

Judy sat down across from me. "I've got so much to talk to you about. I've been looking into different tax structures for the business, and I've got some ideas. I mean, first I thought we should go nonprofit, but that gets too much attention from the IRS. So I'm thinking..."

Oh, hell no, I thought, panic rising in my throat. I actually stood up. *Maybe I need to go unpack? Alone in my room?*

To my shock, Judy chuckled. Then her chuckles turned into laughs.

I sat back down.

Now she was gasping and holding-her-sides laughing.

"I'm sorry," she wheezed. "I'm sorry. It's just the look on your face...."

She struggled to stop grinning.

"I promise I'll shut up." She shook her head. "I'll put my recommendations in a memo to you and Mason. Y'all can disagree or ask questions. If I don't hear otherwise, I'll just do it for you. Okay?"

"I think that would be best," I agreed, trying to hold on to at least a few shreds of my dignity.

Judy got up and went into the kitchen. She put down a bowl of water for Skidi and brought me back a Diet Coke.

She sat back down across from me and looked serious.

"Mason won't talk to me right now, so you tell me. Do we have the monster who's been doing all this? Taking all these women?"

"We finally know his name — Winston Bainbridge III. Unfortunately, the man's so rich he's got more top politicians in his pocket than that pedophile creep Jeffry Epstein did. So Mason's seeing how much proof he can uncover.

"But... even more important. We need to find out what happened to Alaska Brown. He sold her somewhere. We go after Bainbridge right now, and it could be years of legal wrangling — if ever — before we find out where she is. Also — if Mason can find the records, maybe we can locate a lot more of the women Bainbridge has sold. And rescue them."

Judy smiled at me. "I'm proud to be a part of this."

Oh crap.

Skidi gave a warning rumble deep in her throat. I turned to her, then looked in the direction she was staring.

A fluffy Persian cat with a bi-colored face — slate blue on one side and white on the other — was standing in the doorway, staring at Skidi. Then at me. She looked appalled. Her gums pulled back, and she gave the loudest hiss I'd ever heard. She turned to Judy with a look that said, "How could you?"

Then she turned around, tail straight up in the air, and stalked away.

Judy and I laughed.

"You hungry?"

I nodded, vigorously. She pulled out her phone and hit the app for the Longhorn Steakhouse. She placed our order, then asked if they could throw in a few bones for a big dog.

The food was delicious. Skidi had grabbed her bones and proceeded to chomp them into pieces on the kitchen floor. I saw her look around, occasionally, to make sure the cat hadn't come back.

Judy was sipping coffee while I had another Diet Coke.

I could see she wanted to ask me something but wasn't sure she should. I half hoped she wouldn't get up the nerve.

"Can I ask you something very personal?" she finally said.

Oh, crap. "You can ask..."

"Why don't you have a man?"

I raised my eyebrows at her.

"I mean, you look great and your personality isn't *too* obnoxious..."

I smiled at that. "Why do you want to know?"

"I don't understand you. I'd like to understand you better."

I thought about it. "I can see that," I told her. "You and men are something. They adore you — their eyes light up and they get all soft around you. And you adore them right back. But it isn't that way for all women. Some of us have trust issues — hard-earned trust issues."

I thought some more. "I'll tell you the real reason, though — as long as you agree to never discuss it again. Agreed?"

She nodded.

"I mean it. Never again."

"I agree."

"I've met the one man I want, but I can't have him. So I'm stuck."

Judy — no surprise — didn't want to leave it at that. "He's married?"

"No, but he will be. And it can't be to me." I sighed. "He's a Lupiti priest. Chiefs come and go, but a priest — he's there for his people for life. As was his father, grandfather, and great-grandfather before him.

So of course he has to marry a Lupiti woman and raise a son. And I'm not Lupiti."

"But..."

I shook my head. "No more."

My cell rang. *Thank god!*

It was Mason. "I found the man who bought Alaska — and three other women. His name is Spencer Z. Johnson, and he owns the biggest animal feed company in the world."

Mason paused. "It's weird, though. He paid $100,000 for Alaska and over $3 million for each of the other three. We knew she didn't fit the profile — but does this mean she's more or less likely to be alive?"

I had no idea.

Mason added, "Even if she's alive, it doesn't mean she's still with Johnson — the sale was almost seven months ago."

"Good work, Mason. Get some sleep."

I called Connor. "We found Alaska. You want in?"

"Try to stop me."

"Saddle up. We're going to Houston."

41

Current Time
Alaska Brown
Location Unknown

Alaska Brown was getting out of this place — whether it killed her or not. She'd been trying to keep the girls and herself alive. And to hold on to the hope of seeing her children again.

But all that changed last night. When Mary Jane Alexander didn't come back from her trip upstairs.

"Miss Brenda" came down the stairs weekly to inspect Alaska's cleaning. Today she made an extra trip down. She told Alaska to clean out Mary Jane's room and prepare it for a new "guest" who would be arriving soon.

"Where's Mary Jane," Alaska asked.

"She's... left us. Gone back home."

Alaska knew they would never let a girl leave here. She saw a tiny flash of disgust in the woman's eyes, and Alaska knew for sure what she'd only suspected last night.

Mary Jane was dead.

Alaska nodded and watched Miss Brenda and armed tat-man go back up the stairs.

Then she went back into her cell and sat on the mattress. And thought.

Each time the past three months that a girl returned from upstairs, Alaska questioned her decision to not help them commit suicide.

The betrayal in Mary Jane's eyes, in particular, had tormented her. And now Mary Jane was dead anyway. She'd got what she wanted, but Alaska could have made it easier for her.

Well... this was it. The next time that bitch came down here to check on her — Alaska was getting out.

In six months, she'd only managed to get and hide a single plastic knife. She'd sharpened it by rubbing it against the smoothest concrete she could find.

She'd slice the neck of tat man — cutting as deep as she could. Then she'd take her chances with Miss Brenda. Use her as a hostage or, if she had to, kill her as well.

She'd take the guard's gun and Brenda's key. She'd let out the two remaining girls and the three of them would go up the stairs.

Or she'd die.

The very next time the bitch came down.

42

A house rented on the Vrbo app
Houston, Texas

It took us six interminable, frustrating days of planning before Connor and I — and Judy — could finally go after Johnson.

We first had to determine where the women were likely held. We tracked his every movement for all six days. Two nights he attended games — an Astros game against the White Sox and a Rockets game against the Celtics. Other than those, the man was either at his office or home. He didn't even go to restaurants but instead had food delivered from the best chefs in town to his home or his office. There were no visits to warehouses where the women might be held.

We reasoned he wouldn't invest $14 million into women he never saw. That left his office or his home.

Connor nixed them being at the office. The CEOs he'd worked for saw their office as part of their kingdom, but they were always aware of their employees. People who could have conflicting loyalties. A secret this big and this bad — they'd see that as too risky.

Johnson's home was where he had the most control. His wife had died 10 years ago and his son owned a small island in the Pacific that he never left. So there was nobody at home to question him.

That left the problem of how to get to him. I couldn't believe all the security measures billionaires take. This one had 100% bulletproof glass windows and cameras everywhere outside the house. He had "burglar blasters" throughout the house that could spray knockout gasses on intruders.

If he suspected trouble, he had a "panic room" he could seal off. Only it wasn't just a room. It was a full bedroom, bath, kitchen, media room, exercise room and a full-length pool. So he didn't have to be inconvenienced while he awaited your arrest.

Or while he sat out the death of the world in the event of a nuclear disaster.

At one point, I joked to Mason that it was too bad the guy didn't fly himself alone in his private jet — so we could shoot him down. "No way," he told me. "His jet has the same $1 million plus anti-missile jamming device used by the U.S. government."

Good grief.

"Although..." Mason said, "I did manage to hack into his plane's computer system. The pilot likes to play Starbase Slayer on it when he's bored."

I shook my head in disbelief.

"How about we get in through one of his live-in help?"

Mason told me there were only three heat signatures in the compound at night — two were on opposite sides of the house, and one was in an apartment above the garage.

We investigated. Johnson had a driver/bodyguard who had to be living above the garage. The other person was Brenda Valle — a woman who was President of the Jebediah G. Johnson Family Foundation, which was named for Johnson's great-grandfather. Valle ran it from an office in Johnson's home. She also had her own living quarters there with a separate entrance.

Two live-in help didn't add up for a billionaire, so I asked Judy about it. She researched and reported back that most of the really rich these days avoid any live-in staff. They use their office personal assistants to manage their houses, including vetted cleaning services, bodyguard services for when they go outside the house, delivery of gourmet restaurant food, and more. She even found a comment in a personal assistant complaint website where one woman bitched about programming Roombas for each room of her boss' house to cut back on the amount of time a cleaning service needed to be in there.

The fewer people in their inner circle — the fewer who could betray them.

Connor was used to analyzing how a person might be kidnapped when outside the house or office. He gave us a couple of options, but I nixed them. A billionaire with only one bodyguard? I was convinced Johnson had several panic-alarm systems in place that could summon more bodyguards or the police. Systems we couldn't count on recognizing.

He for-sure had them for entering his home under duress, and we would have to get him inside the house eventually. Because we had to find the women. Without them — right there as physical proof — there wasn't a law enforcement officer in the country who would even think about searching Johnson's house.

That left Brenda Valle as our best chance. As President of the Foundation, she attended all the high-society charity gatherings in Houston, as well as the biggest ones in Dallas and Fort Worth. She had a rental limo service she used for them, as well as an on-demand bodyguard service.

Grabbing her on the way to or from a charity gala carried too much potential for collateral damage.

She also left the compound most days for a fancy lunch with friends at Potente or Da Marco restaurants, driving herself in her red BMW ix 360. Catching her as she drove home from lunch was our best bet because she was alone. But it was broad daylight, and there were all those outside cameras.

Mason said there were sure to be security procedures at the gate that she could screw us with. A word she could say. Or not say. Using the wrong finger for her fingerprint scan. The wrong eye for a retina scan. So many ways she could drive us into a trap.

Screaming in frustration didn't do any good. I know because I tried it.

Finally, we had a plan.

43

Da Marco restaurant
Houston, Texas

Connor and I got our clothes from the local Neiman Marcus in order to blend in. Because I refused to wear anything with huge flowers on it, I had just two choices in my size — a white suit with a Peter Pan rounded collar or a red sheathe with a black and red geometric jacket.

I went with the red as it was more likely to hide blood.

Judy got a limo-driver outfit of black pants suit, white shirt and a black hat. She had one button too many open on the shirt (of course — it was Judy), and her grey hair stuck out under the hat, framing her face. She looked great in it and said she was keeping it.

We lurked just off Westheimer Road in our rented limo, where we could see the restaurant entrance. When Brenda Valle's BMW pulled in, we gave it 10 minutes then pulled in after her. The closest we could park was three cars away.

Connor and I started to have another fight about who grabs her and who's backup. In exasperation, and because I had no clue which would be better, I told Judy to decide.

"Who," I asked her, "has the best chance of getting to Valle without her hitting an alarm button? The handsome but big-and-maybe-threatening man or the non-threatening-but-uninteresting woman? Who can get closer to her before she panics?"

Judy had seen all the videos of the woman we had — and I suspected her social instincts were better than Connor's or mine.

"Neither," she said. "Be a couple, arm-in-arm happy."

She nodded at me. "You think you recognize her and ask if she isn't the head of some charity. You're impressed."

She nodded at Connor. "You look at her like you're thinking it might be interesting to fuck her. Then, when you hear Sara say she runs a company, you get more interested."

Connor shook his head, looking as confused as I was.

Judy looked dumbstruck. "Y'all are clueless! Look — she's 15 years older than Sara and not as attractive. She's not going to buy love at first sight from Connor. But she would buy him as a hound dog who could give her a fun romp in the sheets. Even better if he's impressed by her status."

Connor and I looked at each other, picturing it.

"You are a genius," I said to Judy. Connor took her hand and made a production out of kissing it.

Connor and I got out of the limo then, and we leaned against it as if we were chit-chatting and flirting. Once Valle came out, we'd be able to reach her car well before she could. Connor had his back to the door, letting me watch for her. When I saw her come out, I took his hand and pulled him forward as though we were going in.

We got just past her car when I pretended to notice her.

"Are you...?"

She looked at me, then her gaze slid to Connor. She must have liked what she saw then because her gaze only came back to me when I added, "You run this really big foundation, don't you? Jeremy Johnson? No, *Jeremiah* Johnson. Yes?"

She nodded at me, but her gaze slid back to include Connor.

I continued, "My daddy is planning to set up a foundation like that. Well... nowhere near as big, but... Do you have a card? Maybe he could call you sometime?"

She didn't reach for a card as I'd hoped she would. Instead, she asked, "Who's your daddy?"

She came to a stop about three feet from us. At the same time, Judy pulled alongside in the limo, stopped, got out, and opened the back door as if for a client.

Thank god nobody else was visible for the moment.

Connor grabbed Valle from the side, his left hand grabbing hers and his right arm circling her waist and lifting her up toward the limo.

I slapped duct tape over her mouth and grasped her right hand — we didn't want her to be able to push or tap an alarm with either hand. Then I followed her and Connor into the back of the limo. We drove three blocks over and pulled into the far part of a medical building parking lot.

Quickly we zip-tied her wrists behind her, and I removed all jewelry, her belt and purse. Connor patted her down to make sure no alarms were hidden in her clothes or shoes. I suddenly remembered Connor's shirt buttons and pointed at hers. He smiled and checked them closely. I ran my fingers through her hair and triple checked around her ears.

Valle and I didn't look at all alike, but our bodies were similar in height and weight. I took her purse, making sure the car fob was inside, and grabbed the wig I'd found that was close to her hairstyle — shoulder length and dark with blond tips.

Brenda wore big jewelry in every picture we saw of her, so I put on her (gorgeous!) turquoise and gold dangle earrings and her chunky turquoise and gold bead necklace.

Connor jabbed Brenda with fast-acting sodium thiopental which, in addition to making her sleepy, would also make her chatty and less careful with what she said.

Judy drove us back to the parking lot entrance to Da Marco's. I got out and waved goodbye at Connor, walked to Brenda's car, got in, thanked the heavens I was able to start it, and drove it away.

The house Judy had rented for us was about two miles from Johnson's compound. As I pulled up to it, Judy passed me in the limo, leaving. She was going to return it to the rental agency and drive back in her own rental car.

I used the garage remote to drive Valle's car inside the garage and out of view. Connor had already set up Valle in one of the bedrooms, tying her legs to the feet of an armchair. Her wrists were still zip-tied behind her. A rag was stuffed in her mouth with a cloth tie around her head, holding the gag in.

Connor and I stood, watching her. We'd agreed on who ran the next step. Connor had grilled people for intel before, but they were terrorists in the field and he was able to stab them to encourage them to talk.

He figured I had more interrogating experience that wouldn't leave wounds. He was right, but... he didn't know my most reliable technique, and I for sure wasn't going to show or tell him.

You'd be amazed at what people will tell you if you can transform your hands into wolf paws with claws or your face into a wolf's snout. I've found one nice, big yawn showing all 42 of my teeth in their sharp, shiny-white glory — and people will tell me anything I want to know.

Unfortunately, I can only do that if I know they're going to die. I can't have lots of people running around screaming I'm a werewolf. Or even one.

Nor am I willing to let Connor or Judy know.

One question with Brenda Valle was whether or not she was in on the whole thing. I was 98% sure she was. No billionaire — sure as hell no billionaire that was buying women so he could do whatever he wanted with them — was going to deal with the day-to-day of having captives. Someone had to feed them, buy Tampax, and clean up after them. Since it wouldn't be Johnson, that left only her or the driver/bodyguard. I figured he was muscle for when that was needed.

"Well, Brenda," I said. "You don't know it yet, but this is the luckiest day of your life."

She snorted.

I pulled up a chair and sat facing her. Close enough to touch her. "Today's the day the shit hits the fan, and Johnson gets carted off in handcuffs. The day you've been dreading for at least —" I pulled out my phone and looked at my notes. "—for at least three years."

She stared at me.

I shrugged. "It might have been longer. But you started at the foundation three years ago, and that's the same time as the first record we've found of Johnson buying a woman."

I looked back at my notes. "Her name was Madison Foster and Johnson paid $3.9 million for her. Four years ago in March."

There was more white showing around Valle's dark brown pupils.

"We also have the records of him buying Hannah Cunningham for $4 million two years ago and buying Mary Jane Alexander for $6.2 million about eight months ago. At the same time as he bought Alaska Brown for a bargain price of $100,000??"

Brenda was shaking her head, left to right.

"There may be more, but these are the names we can prove he bought. We got the records from Winston Bainbridge III. He kept very detailed records of all his sales. The FBI is taking him down today. Probably..." I looked at my watch... "well... not yet. It's planned for 6 PM."

I loved lying to assholes.

"So... you have just four hours before they come for you too."

I nodded at Connor, and he removed the gag. She sputtered and twisted her mouth and coughed.

"Give her a bottle of water," I said. Connor handed her a soft plastic one.

She took two swallows, then gathered herself.

"Now you're a smart woman," I said. "So you've undoubtedly figured the two of us are not with law enforcement. We're private, and we're only here for one woman. The one our client is paying us to rescue.

"Being smart, I suspect you have a bug-out bag all packed and a nice home waiting for you in a non-extradition country. Yes?"

Her face gave me nothing.

"C'mon, Brenda. If you're too stupid to have planned for this — then we have nothing to talk about. We'll just back off and wait for the FBI raid."

I leaned forward to her. "They're raiding Bainbridge and Johnson and two other buyers — all at the same time."

I leaned back. "So, were you smart? Or should we just pack up and leave you here?"

She cleared her throat. "Hypothetically…" she looked at me.

"Hypothetically," I agreed with a nod.

"If I were involved, I would certainly have an escape plan. So who do you want?"

"Alaska Brown."

"Her?" Valle's voice was high, incredulous. That…"

She closed her mouth decisively. But it was too late to pretend she didn't know the woman.

"Is Alaska still alive? Today?"

She nodded.

"Here's how it's going to work."

44

Spencer Z. Johnson's mansion
Houston, Texas

Forty-five minutes later, after Judy got back, we were ready to move.

Judy stayed in the house to make sure we had multiple get-out-of-Houston escape options. She didn't bitch too much about it — she knew what she was doing might be critical.

Connor had to ride in Valle's trunk, which did *not* make him happy. His 6'4", 240 pounds of muscle wouldn't fit in the foot well of the passenger seat. My body did. I couldn't help grinning.

Mason, who was on coms with Judy plus me and Connor, said nothing. But I pictured him grinning along with me.

Valle drove to Johnson's compound, where I ducked into the foot well before she used her card and retina scan to get us into her garage.

After rescuing Connor from the trunk, I stopped us before entering the house.

"Just in case you're having second thoughts... maybe you're thinking Johnson's money can save you...."

Valle just looked at me, not denying anything.

"Just like you have a bug-out plan, think about what Johnson's plan might be. This is in his house, so he has to somehow account for that. Maybe that's why he has you living here? Maybe he's planted some interesting "evidence" about you?"

"That's ridiculous," she said. "The girls would tell—"

"The girls would be dead."

She thought about that. I could see she was making connections with something she'd seen that only now made sense.

I asked, "Do you know how he'd make them dead?"

Her eyes shut down. She said, "The faster we get Alaska the faster I can get out of here."

I nodded. Valle opened the door to the house using a fingerprint scanner. She had said there were no cameras inside the garage or the house. So far, it appeared she was telling the truth.

Connor and I each had a gun out and lying against the side of our legs. We went into Valle's aggressively modern office. Too cold and sterile for me, but it fit her. Although I did like the five brass lights, the size and shape of basketballs, that were hanging over her desk.

Valle reached under the wood slab that was her desk and removed a key. Her hand hesitated by one drawer, then moved away. I opened the drawer and saw a stun gun. I picked it up and added it to the arsenal.

"Log in to your computer," I told her, pointing at the MacBook Pro on the desk.

She hesitated.

Connor placed his automatic against the side of her head.

She opened it and entered a password. I watched. Once she was in, I pulled out a USB-C and plugged it in. I tapped a wolf-puppy pin on my t-shirt. "You in?" I asked Mason.

"Got it," Mason said into my and Connor's ears.

"Let's go," I said to Valle.

She opened the other drawer and handed Connor a remote. "It opens the door to downstairs," she told him.

"If this is a knock-out gas, I'll still have time to kill you," he said, still holding the gun at her head.

"It's not."

205

Connor pushed the button. A section of the wall that looked no different from the rest swung out revealing stairs going down.

"The stairs are from *your* office?" I asked shock evident in my voice. How had she not seen Johnson's Plan B setup?

She motioned for us to go down first.

"No," said Connor. "After you." He moved behind her and pointed his gun at her back.

Worried about getting back out of this dungeon, I pulled two books from the bookcase and jammed the door open. I was *not* getting trapped down there.

The three of us went down. And down. Two flights. They dead ended at a door, which Valle unlocked with her key.

45

Basement of Spencer Z. Johnson's mansion
Houston, Texas

The door opened onto a concrete hallway with three doors opening on the left, two doors and a kitchenette alcove on the right, and a single door at the end of the hall.

Valle started forward, past the first doors, but Connor stopped her by grabbing her arm.

I grabbed the first door on the right. Inside I found a little cleaning closet with mop, vacuum, cleaning solutions, rags and paper towels.

The first door on the left was locked. There was a window with bars in it. I saw a bedroom with no furniture except for a bed, chair and chest of drawers. There was a bathroom beyond it with no door. There was a mound in the bed as if someone were sleeping there with the covers pulled over her head.

"Key," I said to Valle.

She shook her head, said, "Alaska's down at the end," and jerked her arm away from Connor. He let her go.

We passed a kitchenette, which had everything except a stove or oven. There wasn't even a hot plate, but there was a microwave. The next door on the left was also locked, the inside identical to the first, except the woman sleeping in the bed showed a mass of black curls on the pillow.

"She's the last door on the right," said Valle.

The last door on the left was locked, but the room was stripped bare of linens. Nobody there.

The last door on the right showed a very different looking room — a concrete cell with a hole in the floor for a toilet. A woman with short dark hair that had been hacked off with scissors looked at us through the window.

It was Alaska Brown.

My heart stopped. I realized, deep down, I had never expected to find her alive.

I turned to Connor and pointed at me and then at Alaska's cell. I pointed at him and the final door at the end of the hall.

He nodded.

"Then," I said, "get back upstairs and work with..." I tapped my earpiece, "...on whoever else is in this compound. Don't let us get trapped down here."

Connor turned to the last door, but Valle grabbed his arm. "It won't open that door. I was told to never go in there."

Connor and I frowned at each other.

I tried Alaska's door and found it wasn't locked. I pushed it open and shoved Valle in the room with me.

"Alaska Brown," I said. "Your parents hired me to find and rescue you."

I had pictured this moment for weeks now, trying to convince myself it could happen. But it was nothing like what I imagined. There was no joy — or relief — on her face. Instead, she stared hard at me with narrowed eyes.

I tried again. "We should get out of here."

She looked at Valle with bone-deep hatred and said to me, "You're working with her?"

"Let's just say..." I started.

Valle interrupted me. "My God," she said to Alaska. "You're even stupider than I thought. Let's go... unless you want to stay here."

Connor's head appeared in the door, and he motioned at me to join him. When I stepped out into the hall, he closed Alaska's door and handed me Valle's key.

"The key doesn't work. Nor my lock pick. Mason says the door is loaded with electronics — if I break in, it might blow up."

"Then skip it. Go on up and make sure we're clear to get out...."

The look on Connor's face shut me up. "Oh shit," he said, looking over my shoulder into Alaska's room.

I felt a flash of nausea and turned. Alaska and Valle were standing together, and a gush of blood was covering them both.

"Go," I said to Connor, nodding back to the stairs.

As I threw open Alaska's door, the two women separated. Valle sank to her knees, then fell to her side. Alaska backed away — holding a small bloody knife. She'd cut a slash across Valle's neck that was now pumping her blood out as fast as her heart could beat.

Valle was already unconscious. She'd be dead in 15-20 more seconds.

"Are you hurt?" I asked Alaska.

She held her knife up in front of her as though threatening me next.

"Are. You. Hurt?"

"No." She shook her head.

"Good." I started breathing again. I pulled out my Spyderco knife from my boot and chopped off Valle's left hand.

Alaska backed away from me in horror. "What are you doing?"

"Take this." I shoved Valle's dripping hand to Alaska, who emphatically shook her head no. I grabbed her arm and stuck the hand in Alaska's. "We may need her fingerprint to get the hell out of this place. You killed her. You bring the hand. Actions have consequences."

Tears welled in her eyes. I mentally kicked myself and sighed. "Just like Valle's actions carried consequences for her."

I stepped forward and put an arm on her shoulder. She let me.

"C'mon," I said. "Let's rescue the two women here and get the hell out."

I opened the cell door and held it for Alaska. She came out, holding Valle's hand as far away from her as possible.

The key opened both other cell doors, and Alaska ran into each. She shook each girl awake, carefully hiding the hand behind her. She told them they were being rescued. To come right now while they could. She pushed and prodded, and soon they were both behind me — going up the stairs. Alaska brought up the rear.

I was almost to the door at the top when I heard a loud crash. A body slammed into the door, splintering part of it. I saw cowboy boots scramble to get upright and then charge across the room. Another slam followed.

Motioning for the women to stay put, I moved up the stairs and got my first look at what was going on.

It was a knife fight. Connor and the muscle guy from the garage — Tank — who was appropriately named because he matched Connor's 6' 4" and then some.

It made no sense. Where was his gun?

My eyes searched and found two automatics slammed up against the wall near me.

I thought about picking them up. Or trying to help Connor.

But I just stood there. Paralyzed by a sight I'd never seen before. Bodies were spinning. Blades were flashing so fast they were blurs.

How could Connor even *see* the man's knife, much less protect against it?

My gun hung useless in my hand. I brought it up, but they moved so fast and kept spinning. First, Tank had his back to me. Then Connor. Then Tank.

It was like a dance. A crazy, lethal dance where death jumped back and forth with mad glee. Cackling, delighting in a moment in time when everything was literally on a knife's edge. Where every second foretold victory or death. Or even both.

It was the most beautiful, horrible, can't-breathe thing I'd ever seen.

Then Tank lunged and Connor turned slightly, almost like a matador. The knife slid past Connor's chest, brushing his shirt as it passed. Still in the half spin away, Connor's knife hand came around and hit the man in the back of the neck.

Burying the knife.

Connor kicked him hard in the back, pulling the knife back out and sending him slamming into the floor. Face down. His right leg twitched a couple of times and then lay still.

Connor turned and nodded at me, his chest gulping air.

During his fight, he had actually seen me, registered me, and then dismissed me as a problem. Without losing a second of focus.

"Holy crap!" I said, then winced. I sounded way too fan girl.

"Agreed," he said, shaking his head. "It's been too long — he almost got me."

He pulled up his shirt and I saw a serious gash on his side. I noticed he was dripping blood. Leaving DNA.

Suddenly there was screaming in my ear. Mason.

"Get out of there now. Bomb!"

46

Spencer Z. Johnson's mansion
Houston, Texas

Connor and I met eyes. I ran for the door to the basement and screamed for the women to come as fast as they could. I threw one of the women to Connor, grabbed another with Alaska, and we ran for the door.

"Bomb!" I yelled to speed up the women.

We hit the garage as I heard a rumbling from the house. Connor had his woman in the front and was behind the wheel. I shoved the other two in the back and jumped in on top of them.

There was a crack explosion and the car shook. A concrete beam holding up the wall shifted and partially crumbled.

"Fuck!" Connor hit the gas while the car doors were still open. The garage door was in sight when Connor jerked the wheel left to avoid a chunk of concrete landing where we would have been.

He jerked the wheel back and pointed us at the garage door.

"Umm," I said, wondering if he really thought this sports car could break through a fortified garage door. We were 20 feet away when there was a noise and growing light showed under the door. It opened quickly, telling me we must have tripped a beam that opened it.

Guess Johnson wasn't worried about people getting *out* of his house.

We were barely passed the door when a horrible boom announced the explosion of the entire house. Shrapnel-sounding pellets hit the back of the car. A big chunk of something hit the car top and bounced off, leaving a dent right over my head.

As we turned a corner to where the gate was, I looked at Alaska's hands. They were empty.

"We've got no fingerprint for security," I yelled to Connor.

He strained, trying to press the pedal even farther to the floor. But we were already full-out.

Up ahead, I saw a Range Rover flying through the open gate.

"Gotta be Johnson," I said. "Mason, keep eyes on his Range Rover."

"Got him," I heard in my ear. "And Judy will be there in two minutes."

The heavy iron gate started to slide back in, closing.

Closing.

We were too late.

"Brace yourself," Connor yelled.

He had no chance to get through it, but he hit it on the edge going at least 60.

Billionaires can pay for the best, and this one had. We went from 60 to zero in a nanosecond. The crash was ear-splitting, and I felt like... Well... Like I'd been in a car doing 60 when it hit a wall.

When I came to, my whole body ached.

I checked the women and panicked. Alaska had blood coming from her mouth.

"Are you okay?"

"My tongue! I bit it. Ow!"

I gasped in relief.

The hood of the car was up, blocking our vision. I tried my car door, and it worked. I staggered out, and the two women followed me.

Amazingly the gate had been pushed out enough it could no longer close. It left a gap that we could squeeze through.

There was kicking as Conor tried to open his door. Then he crawled over the seat to the back, bringing the other girl. They got out behind us.

I rushed us through the opening quickly, just in case. Miraculously nobody seemed hurt, beyond bruising.

"We got lucky," I said.

Connor shook his head. "Top-of-the-line BMW. Good crash test results."

An SUV came into view. Judy was here.

"Mason?" I asked into my wolf-puppy pin.

"Not sure yet," he said, "but I think Johnson's heading to the David Wayne airport and his jet."

Oh, hell!

"Get everyone in the car," I yelled. "He can't get to the airport, or he's gone."

Judy got out and helped.

I turned to Connor. "How's your run-somebody-off-the-road driving skills?"

"Great." His look convinced me.

"You drive. Let Mason guide you on which roads to take."

The three of us piled in with the three women, and Connor hit the gas.

"Judy..." I turned to her.

She was on the phone, saying, "I need to rent a six-seat van for about a week. Can you deliver it to the David Wayne airport now — I'll be there in 20 minutes?"

I shook my head and smiled. She was always a step ahead of me. A van made sense. We were a seven-hour drive to Tulsa — much smarter than going by plane. And a week gave us time to return it.

Then I caught a glimpse of the houses outside the car. They were moving by so fast they were a blur. I closed my eyes, not wanting to see. Connor had the "fast" part of driving down pat. I only hoped he was also good at the "staying alive" part.

Think, Sara, I told myself. *What's next?*

Oh yes, deniability.

I turned to Alaska. "We would appreciate being kept out of this — to whatever extent you feel comfortable doing. Please don't describe us — say we were wearing masks.

"Most important — say one of us killed the woman who kept you imprisoned. That's how you were able to rescue the other girls and get out."

The SUV spun around a turn and threw me on top of Alaska. I started to say something smart to Connor, but I shut my mouth and refused to look outside to see how we were doing. He was mumbling to Mason over a separate link.

Alaska looked at me and shook her head. "No," she said. "I killed her. I won't blame someone else."

"Do you want the law to victimize you all over again?"

She scrunched her face in resolve, not giving an inch.

I tried to calm down. I tried another tactic. "Okay, listen. Everyone is entitled to a lawyer, right?"

She nodded cautiously.

"Judy," I nodded my head at her. "Judy is going to give you and your parents the name of an attorney who is very good. He's on retainer with us so you won't need to pay him. Don't do anything until you talk to him."

I put my hands on her shoulders and stared at her. "Promise me."

She thought. Then she nodded. "I promise."

Connor hit the brakes, and my head slammed into the front seat back.

For a second, I saw two of Alaska. Then she merged back into one.

We needed more seat belts in the back of this SUV — I'd got them around everyone else but me. But if somebody's brains had to be scrambled, better it was mine. Because mine could be fixed.

Probably.

"Judy's going to call him — his name is Atticus Snowden — and have him pick you and the other two up. He'll put you somewhere safe, get you fed and rested. Then he'll help you each come up with a plan. You're going to need him to protect all three of you. From the police and the press. And from any pals of the man who bought the three of you.

"The man who owned that house?" asked Alaska.

I nodded.

"What is his name?"

"Spencer Johnson. He's the man we're chasing right now."

Alaska's eyes narrowed, and she stared out of the front window.

Connor yelled at me. "He's right ahead. What do you want?"

I leaned forward in my seat, my mouth at Connor's ear.

"Where's the airport?"

"Right up ahead." He jerked his chin, and I saw the entrance about a block away.

Connor said, "I'd pull alongside, but he's sure to have bullet-proof glass and tires."

"We're too late," I said, shaking my head in despair. "He's had too much time to make phone calls. He'll have bodyguards there."

Connor lowered his voice and said, "He'll get away with this, you know. With his money..."

"I know." I closed my eyes.

"Shit!" Connor pounded the steering wheel.

In my ear, I heard Mason say, "I can crash his plane."

"What?" Connor and I both asked the same thing.

"I'm in his system. I can shut it down in mid-air."

Connor slowed down to the speed limit and looked at me in the rearview mirror.

Mason continued, "You can't get him on the ground. He'll have security all over the airport."

"But..." Connor started. I shook my head at him in the rear viewmirror, and he closed his mouth.

"Let's go to the airport," I said, "and park at one of the commercial buildings there. We can see who gets on the plane."

Connor nodded slowly in the mirror.

Three minutes later, we pulled into the airport. There were two black GMC Yukons parked next to a Range Rover. The doors were open and one well-armed man was standing by them.

As we pulled to a hanger, a building away, we saw seven armed men escorting Johnson to a jet — a huge one for a private plane. Johnson went up the stairs and the door closed behind him. The seven men relaxed their body posture and walked back to the vehicles. The jet taxied down the runway and took off.

"That's a Gulfstream G650," said Connor. "It's the holy grail of executive jets — Bezos and Musk both have them."

"That's his," Mason said into our ears. "They've filed a flight plan down to Nevis in the Caribbean."

"Everyone stay here," I said. "Connor and I need to talk."

Connor and I got out of the car and closed the doors. Judy got out as well. I'd forgotten she could hear Mason along with Connor and me.

She put her hands on our arms and said, softly, "I've been talking to Alaska. You don't want to know what Johnson did to these women, but burning in hell would be too good for him."

"I'd say kill him," said Connor, "but how many other people are on the plane?"

"Don't hesitate based on the pilot," Mason told us. "This guy is his special pilot. I checked the service, and this is the guy who flew his jet to Houston right after Johnson bought each of the women."

The two Yukons, now packed with four men each, left the airport.

I looked at Connor. "Johnson might have a bodyguard on the plane with him."

Connor nodded. "He might. But he was alone in that Land Rover. And the eight emergency guys didn't go with him."

"He blew up his home," I said. "It was always his backup plan to blow up the girls to hide his crimes."

We all looked at each other. Would we really do this?

Mason said in our ears, "He's over the Gulf of Mexico now. You need to decide in the next 10 minutes, or he might be able to find a place to land."

Connor and Judy stared at me.

I shook my head. "I'm not deciding this one alone. It would affect all of us."

Judy: "If he wasn't a billionaire, I'd say let the law take care of him. But billionaires... they never face justice."

Mason: "If he realizes he can't escape, he could just kill himself. Like that pedophile Jeffrey Epstein did."

Connor: "Only, he won't have to if it goes to a higher court judge, one of his "close personal friends" he's been paying off in half-million-dollar vacations... or he'll buy the dictator of a country that won't extradite him."

"Votes?" I asked.

"Do it," said Connor and Mason.

"Kill him," said Judy.

"Mason," I asked. "You'll just turn off the plane? He won't die instantly, right? He'll have some time to see it coming?"

"Probably 3-5 minutes."

"Good. He doesn't deserve to die instantly."

"Done," said Mason.

All three of us standing there took deep breaths.

I said, "Let's get out of here. Let's get that van and get on the road to Tulsa and get these women to Atticus."

Judy pulled out her phone. As we got back in the SUV, I heard her say, "Atticus, sweetie? We're bringing you some new clients."

As we pulled away, I said, "Mason, let's see what the feds can do against Winston Bainbridge III. Drop a tip to that FBI Special Agent in Charge. Give him the scoop on what Johnson and Bainbridge were up to. Send him a copy of the records you got from Bainbridge's files."

"Agreed. Let's see if he can become one billionaire to face justice for his crimes."

47

Two months later
Sara's House
Tulsa Oklahoma

It was funny how much I looked forward to throwing this party. I was never a party girl, but...

When Mason and I solved our first case after I became a P.I. — saving Lillian Knudsen's life — she threw a party for the five of us. I was surprised at how much I enjoyed it. It made a great conclusion to the worry and the danger of the case.

So I decided to throw one now that Alaska and the two women with her were home safe, and five more women had been found and rescued. One of those five women was the real Brittany Rebane — who told everyone the "I'm running away with my boyfriend" story because she didn't want anyone to know she was gay. Only the male "friend" who volunteered to pick her up — sold her instead.

Most important for the celebration — Spencer Johnson was dead, and Winston Bainbridge III had just been indicted.

My modest-sized ranch house sits on a spit of land surrounded on three sides by the meandering Arkansas River. I love the river, even though Mason once said it looked like I was surrounded by a river of sludge.

Muddy is *not* the same as sludge.

I looked out the patio doors and saw Mason firing up my grill — under the watchful eyes of Skidi. He had steak, corn on the cob, and some skewers of vegetables all prepped and waiting for the coals to get hotter.

The doorbell rang and I opened it to greet Connor and Lillian. I'd introduced them when I hired Connor to help me bodyguard Lillian. After the case, they'd both decided they liked what they'd seen. I was delighted they were still together.

I was also amazed that she hadn't told him my secret. I'd had to transform when I saved her from a bombing. Lillian and Mason, and a Lupiti priest named Bill, were the only three who knew what I was. When I found out she and Connor were dating, I was so sure my secret would be out that I'd bought 50 acres in the middle of Tennessee under an assumed name and moved an RV on it. I'd had a go-bag packed for the last... hell, almost a year now. Ready to disappear.

But I hadn't had to. I was really grateful for that.

It was a perfect night in mid-June — the temperature had dropped to a chilly 70, which meant we could both grill and sit around a fire pit without risking heat stroke.

I stepped back inside when I got a phone call from Carmen, who was keeping that name. Atticus Snowden liked her, so after she told her all to the Feds, he got her a work visa to do translating for his office. We chatted for a few minutes. She was all excited because Atticus just told her he'd pay for her to go paralegal school.

I smiled as I hung up. Then I walked back outside and re-joined the party, plunking down in one of the plastic Adirondack chairs circling my fire pit.

We ate and we talked about... nothing really. The weather — how it was supposed to hit 100 next week. How the Mets were looking good this year (okay, that was just me). Why the Oklahoma Thunder was so bad and how dumping James Hardin ages ago was the beginning of the end for them.

Nine at night came and went, and the light left the sky. We were still talking.

Judy changed the tone when she wondered if Bainbridge would really go down for his crimes. He was claiming he had no idea about the operation — that it was all run by his money manager, a man named Liam Mitchell. A man who just happened to eat his pistol the night after Connor and I saved Alaska and the two other women.

"They'll never convict Bainbridge," Connor said for the umpteenth time. "He's too rich and his friends are too powerful. If this faked suicide of his manager doesn't get him off, he'll invent something else. It makes me sick."

I agreed that Liam Mitchell wasn't a suicide. Mason had seen evidence incriminating the man magically appear in Bainbridge's files right after Johnson died when his plane crashed in the Gulf of Mexico.

I'd told Mason to stay out of the files now that the feds were crawling all over them.

Judy was more concerned about Alissa Barnett, the Osage maid who'd gone missing 11 months before Alaska. We hadn't found anything about her. Mason ran into a complete dead end, and none of us could find another lead. But I knew Mason would keep revisiting it. Trying to find something.

I got up to get some ice cream from the fridge for dessert. When I brought out the bowls, I had to smile at Connor and Lillian — sitting out there hand-in-hand and smiling at each other.

Later, Judy and Mason leaned together. It looked like she was trying to wheedle something out of him. I picked up the dishes and took them back in the house. As I was dumping them in the sink I saw, out the window, Judy jump up, looking appalled. She turned and stomped into the house.

She came face-to-face with me and took a deep breath. She unclenched her hands.

"Mason says y'all are planning to dump me. Because you're afraid that I'll get hurt. Is this true?"

Oh boy.

"I wouldn't say dumping..."

"Are you going to hire me again for the next case?"

"Well…"

"This sucks! I'm the best person you could find for this job."

"I agree. Judy, you're fantastic. I'm in awe of your work. Anyone would be very lucky to have you. But you could have *died*."

She looked at me. "Could you have died on this case?"

I shook my head. "That's different."

"Could you have died?"

"Yes," I admitted.

"What if I tell you to stop taking any cases where you could die?"

I shook my head harder. "That's different."

"The hell it is!"

She was furious. She had to be — I'd never once heard her swear before. And she was yelling — she never yelled.

"You're going to keep doing it because you can make a difference. You saved eight women. And you'll save more. Even if you risk your life. Well, I have the right to make the same decision."

She took a breath and lowered her voice. "Do you know how rare it is to find a job where you can make a difference? I spent my whole life fixing houses and making fancier parties for people. And it was okay. It was fine.

"Then you drop in my life, and suddenly I'm saving women from *torture*. These women don't need a better party — they need to stop being abused. They need freedom from slavery.

"And I helped them. Okay, not as direct as y'all. But I got you out of Mexico. I got you the drone so you could rescue Connor and find those women."

She shook her head at my not getting it. "I'm not going back to what I did before. And you can't make me. I'll sit outside your office door downtown and make a huge scene."

She took a breath. "And, by the way, what do you think about 'Last Chance Investigations' for your business name?"

"Huh?"

"You need a name. You can't keep having a blank door with no name on it. People will be afraid to bring you their cases — afraid you're not professional."

I put my hands over my face and rubbed my eyes. "Judy..."

"You can't keep me away. I'll fly a plane over your house trailing one of those banner things saying, 'Hire Judy.' I'll make the biggest pest of myself you can imagine..."

I heard a smothered laugh behind my back.

I turned. Mason had come up behind me and had heard her whole rant. I gave him a "Help me" look, but he shook his head.

"I agree with Judy. You know we need her badly. And if she wants to risk her life to do something that matters to her — well, that's her decision. Besides... you really *don't* want to see how big a pest she can make of herself — do you? I sure don't."

He shuddered dramatically.

I stared at him and then her. I closed my eyes. Then I opened them and took her right hand in mine and shook.

"You're hired. We desperately need you. But you can't stop me from worrying about you."

Judy grinned from ear to ear. "That's okay. You worrying about me is kinda cute. But you're not my mommy."

"Thank God," I muttered under my breath quietly. But not quietly enough.

Mason grinned and slapped me on the back. "Now you've got the spirit. One down, one more to go. Right?" He raised his chin to point outside where Connor and Lillian still were.

Horrified, I turned to him. "What?"

"You know we're better with both of them. So buck up and go ask him."

"You ask him," I said, sounding whiny even to me. "*Partner*."

Mason grinned even bigger, raising both hands and backing away. "People stuff is *your* job — partner."

I really wanted to go bang my head against a wall. But Mason had a point. If we were hiring Judy — and somehow we just did — then it made zero sense to not hire Connor. After all, people try to kill him all the time and he's still alive.

I stepped outside and took a moment to gather myself. I loved the night and the bonfire. And being with people who meant something to me.

Connor and Lillian turned to look at me. I walked on over. "Can I borrow Connor for a couple of minutes?"

"Sure," Lillian said. "I was about to go hit the restroom, anyway." She got up, and Connor did as well.

Lillian gave me a look. "You two play nice together."

I raised my hands in surrender and gave my best "Who me?" look.

She turned to look at Connor, who gave a grin and drawled, "Darlin', I always play nice." She shook her head smiling and walked away.

"I really like her," I said, watching Lillian go.

"I do too," he said. "So what's up?"

"Judy's joining our team — full time."

"Great — it's what she wants. But I thought you wanted to be the Lone Ranger."

I sighed. "I really did. I still do. But we're much better with her. We can do so much more good."

I looked down — this was even harder than I'd expected. I forced myself to look him in the eyes.

"That brings us to you, Connor. We're much better with you, too. I know you had doubts, but let me make you an offer."

He tilted his head, listening.

"If you want to join us full-time — we'd love to have you. And we'd have enough for you to do. In between cases, Judy said you offered to teach her some self defense. And you know I want you to train me.

"If you want to keep body guarding or anything else and only want to work with us occasionally — that would be fine too. We're better with you, Connor. We'll take you however it works for you."

He frowned at me. "This is a weird job offer. What about money?"

"We'd pay you more than you're making now."

"You don't know what I'm making now."

"It doesn't matter — we'd pay you more. You know how risky this work is. We won't nickel and dime you."

Connor looked down. "I'll think about it. Probably not full-time. But give me a call when you get the next case."

"Fair enough."

He turned to walk back toward the house.

"Connor?"

He turned back. I said, "After each case, Mason and I like to make a small donation to a charity that really matters to each of us. Do you have a charity like that?"

He nodded. "I volunteer with the Wounded Warrior Project. Only 5% of their donations go to administrative fees."

"Done."

48

94 Days Later
Last Chance Investigations office
Tulsa, Oklahoma

It was almost October — I didn't know where September had gone.

I was sitting in my revamped — thanks to Judy — office with my cowboy boots up on my Salvation Army crappy desk, which I'd refused to let her replace.

I was reading an article on the *Tulsa World* website about the suspicious suicide of Winston Bainbridge III.

According to *Tulsa World*, Bainbridge had been found in his Phoenix home with a self-inflicted gunshot to his temple. He'd left a note admitting he was the power behind the female trafficking operation he'd blamed on his dead assistant.

According to the newspaper, Bainbridge's death was suspicious because the Phoenix D.A. announced last week they would not charge him in the operation. All evidence pointed to his assistant running it.

Also suspicious — a glitch had turned off the security alarms at Bainbridge's house one hour before his death. And two armed security guards stationed outside the house had apparently been drugged.

The article concluded by saying the FBI was looking into it.

I smiled. The FBI would never be able to find out how Mason had disabled the system.

I smiled even bigger remembering the looks on Bainbridge's face. The arrogance as he told me that nothing would make him write a suicide note. The stark terror as I transformed my face to wolf, and told him just what would happen to him if he didn't. In the end, he was happy to write the note.

My reading was interrupted by a knock on the door, followed by Connor just barging in. I hadn't seen the man in three months, but he looked the same — short reddish blond hair on a body built like a Mack truck.

He stood there, just inside the doorway, looking at me.

"You hear about Bainbridge?" he asked.

I pointed at the article on my computer screen and said, "Just now."

I made a tsk tsk noise. "Guess the man had a guilty conscious after all."

He kept looking at me. "You didn't have anything to do with his sudden change of heart, did you?"

"Me?" I widened my eyes in a picture of innocence. "Of course not." I stared at him.

He stared back at me. Then he nodded. "Of course not."

He closed the door and sat down on one of the comfortable blue chairs Judy had bought and placed facing my desk.

"Shit — why didn't you take me with you?"

Deadpan, I said, "I have no idea what you're talking about."

Connor crossed his legs, looking casual. But the pose was a lie.

"I..." he stopped. Took a breath. Appeared to change what he was going to say. "My friend at Wounded Warriors says they got a $1,000 donation in my name the day after we talked at your house."

I nodded.

"They also got a $1 million anonymous donation that same day. Know anything about that?"

"Of course not. But... good for them. I understand they're a good cause."

"Sara," he said slowly. "Where does your money come from?"

I stared back at him. "Why do you want to know?"

"Because I can't work with some group funded by those working against the United States."

I raised my eyebrows in shock that he would suspect such a thing. But then I nodded. Black money could be from anywhere. He was right to be concerned.

"That guy we took out in Texas — Spencer Johnson?"

He nodded.

"The man left an estate of $106 billion. We didn't touch a cent of that. But Mason found a piddly $14 million account he had buried in a dummy corporation in the Caribbean. He probably had a lot more hidden, but that's all we found. We took that. He's one of our 'donors.'"

A slow grin spread over Connor's face. "A 'donor,' huh?"

I smiled back at him. "We take a lot of pleasure in how pissed our donors would be to know their money went both to charities and to stopping more entitled, murdering assholes just like them."

"This operation is really big, isn't it?"

I shook my head. "No. It's actually very small. Just Mason, Judy and me. And — maybe you?"

"Small in people. But with that amount of money, you can go after powerful bad guys. Not just the ordinary assholes that usually go down. You can do a huge amount of good."

He looked into my eyes. "You still want me to join you?"

"Very much so."

"Then I'm in. What do we do next?"

"Fantastic!"

There was a knock on my door, then it opened.

Bill Hanalho stood in the doorway — the Lupiti priest who had to marry a Lupiti woman to carry on his family's line.

I found myself standing. *You're not Lupiti*, I reminded myself — forcefully.

Because I had forgotten just how good the man looked. The long, black hair hanging halfway to his waist. The eyes that pulled at me like black holes. And the body. Six feet of Western male in well-worn blue jeans and boots. A light blue flannel shirt — that looked softer than a cloud — covered what I knew to be the finest-looking male chest I'd ever seen.

My mouth was dry, and I tried to swallow.

"Sara," he said.

"Bill."

Silence hung between us.

Out of the corner of my eye, I noticed movement. Connor rose from his chair and was looking from me to Bill.

It occurred to me I should introduce them.

I heard Connor say, "I reckon there's something I need to do." He looked like he was suppressing a smile. "I'll call you tomorrow."

I shook my head to focus. "Good idea," I said to him.

"Nice to meet you," Connor said to Bill, the smile growing into a big grin. Then he walked outside the door and closed it.

"Sara," Bill said. "I... there's a woman who needs you. It's about her father. You're the only one who has any chance of helping her."

It took me a second to decipher his words. "A client, you mean... sure."

I sat back down behind my desk. I couldn't be disappointed. After all, this was what I did.

"Have a seat and tell me about her."

∼

MORE DANGER for Sara and her team of misfits! A young woman disappears while seeking evidence her father was murdered 12 years ago — instead of dying drugged and stupid in a Wyoming snowstorm. But to do that, Sara has to confront a man who even U.S. presidents have been afraid to touch. Grab your copy of Murder in Yellowstone, Book 3 in the Sara Flores, Werewolf P.I. series.

FREE STORY DOWNLOAD
NOT AVAILABLE IN ANY STORE!

Werewolves and Holidays

Sometimes I write poor Sara Flores into a corner and even I can't figure out how she's going to survive. That's when I take a week off and write a short story. Typically about a case involving her and some holiday.

I offer the story exclusively to anyone who joins my monthly author mailing list. (It's not available elsewhere.)

You can get your free story by going to: SueDenver.com. Right on the home page there will be a story for the current holiday and a signup to get it for free. Which holiday? You won't know until you check it out!

ABOUT THE AUTHOR

Did you ever want to be more than yourself? I always have. As a kid, I imagined I lived up in the clouds with a band of other kids. We would swoop down — because we could fly! — and rescue people in trouble. And we'd beat the crap out of their abusers.

When I got older, I became obsessed with crime and mysteries. I wanted to know how someone could track down evil doers and expose them to the world.

The day I quit my corporate job — my dreams came true. Today I spend my days throwing my character, Sara Flores, at one criminal mastermind after another — just to see what she can do.

And... I cheated. I let her be more than herself by making her a werewolf — the only magical creature in a world otherwise just like ours. Because I wanted to see what she could do with a wolf's senses and strength. And wildness.

So join me for stories of ruthless criminals, suspicious cops, and Sara's small band of misfits fighting to save us all. Test drive my world with a free story at SueDenver.com.

ALSO BY SUE DENVER

Available now at your favorite booksellers

BOOK 1: SARA FLORES, WEREWOLF P.I. SERIES: Will her first case be her last? Lillian Knudsen, a war vet and amputee, has someone out to kill her. Werewolf Sara Flores got her P.I. license for one reason — to give cops an excuse why they might find her near dead bodies. It turns out evildoers who attack innocents aren't interested in giving them up without a fight. But Sara can't say to to Lillian, and soon she's up to her snout in hired assassins and explosives — because money is no object to the man who wants Lillian — and now Sara too — dead.
[Novella - 146 Pgs.]

BOOK 3, SARA FLORES, WEREWOLF P.I. SERIES: *Sara Flores, werewolf P.I., needs to find a young woman who disappeared seeking evidence her father was murdered 12 years ago — instead of dying drugged and stupid in a Wyoming snowstorm. But to do that, Sara has to confront a man who even U.S. presidents have been afraid to touch.*
[Novel]

BOOK 1: WOLFLADY SERIES. *Abandoned. Nobody to show her the ropes. How will she use her new powers? Nobody believes werewolves exist. Neither did Sara Flores until her Lupiti neighbor turned her. He then had the unmitigated gall to die on her, before telling her anything about what to expect. Sara determines to use her new skills for good. But besides saving innocents, what exactly does that mean? Yes, she can track down bullies and evildoers. But, is it okay to kill them? If so, is it okay to eat them? How about if she's really, really hungry?*
[Collection: All 7 WolfLady short stories plus one novella — Curiosity Kills. 214 pgs.]

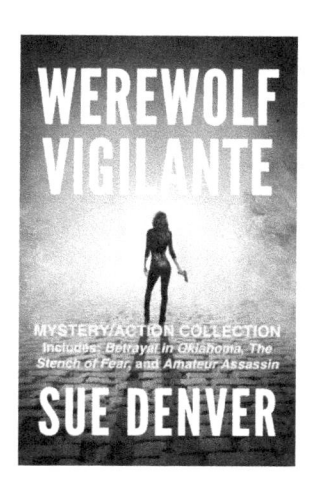

BOOK 2: WOLFLADY SERIES: Payback is a bitch! 3 werewolf vigilante novellas in one boxed set. Rescuing those in need isn't all Sara Flores likes about her new life as a werewolf. Who knew it would be so much fun terrorizing evil doers? The looks on their faces when they discover they're not invincible — it just warms a girl's heart. Set includes: **Betrayal in Oklahoma, Amateur Assassin,** *and* **The Stench of Fear.** *[210 Pgs.]*

ACKNOWLEDGMENTS

A special thanks to my lifelong friend, Vallerina Day, for meeting me at a casino in North Carolina, so I could research what casinos are like these days. And for advising me on Guadalajara businesses, because she lived near there for several years.

She and I first met in college. We became roommates there after the ones we'd each been assigned hated us and wanted to dump us — for which I'm eternally grateful as they probably would have bored each of us to death(!)

Also great thanks to my sister Gloria Ginn who has always encouraged my writing, even when a couple of friends thought I was crazy. Her enthusiasm keeps me going when I write Sara into so much trouble that I am completely befuddled how to get her out of it. "You'll figure it out," she tells me. And, somehow, I do. Thank you!